HENRY

HENRY

BREAKING THE PATTERN #1

P.D. WORKMAN

ISBN: 9781774682029 (IS Hardcover)

ISBN: 9781774682012 (IS Paperback)

ISBN: 9781774682036 (IS Large Print)

ISBN: 9781774681985 (KDP Paperback)

ISBN: 9781774681992 (Kindle)

ISBN: 9781774682005 (ePub)

pdworkman

ALSO BY P.D. WORKMAN

Breaking the Pattern:

Henry

Sandy

Bobby

Between the Cracks:

Ruby

June and Justin

Michelle

Chloe

Ronnie

June, Into the Light

Tamara's Teardrops:

Tattooed Teardrops

Two Teardrops

Tortured Teardrops

Vanishing Teardrops

Medical Kidnap Files:

Mito

EDS

Proxy

Toxo

Pain

Stand Alone YA novels

Stand Alone

Don't Forget Steven

Those Who Believe

Cynthia has a Secret

Questing for a Dream

Darkness before the Dream (prequel story)

Once Brothers

Intersexion

Making Her Mark

Endless Change

Gem, Himself, Alone

MYSTERY/SUSPENSE:

Parks Pat Mysteries

Out with the Sunset

Long Climb to the Top

Dark Water Under the Bridge

Stand Alone Suspense Novels

Looking Over Your Shoulder

Lion Within

Pursued by the Past

In the Tick of Time

Loose the Dogs

AND MORE AT PDWORKMAN.COM

*For all those who struggle to stay on the
straight and narrow*

1

———————

Henry tried to enter the room quietly and remain inconspicuous. Sort of hard when the class was silent for a lecture and he arrived halfway through the period. The blackboard was already full of notes students were copying into their binders. He scanned the room for an empty desk and hoped the one he chose was actually free and not just empty because someone had gone to the restroom or was sick that day. He slipped in as quietly as possible, praying that the teacher would just keep going. But Mrs. Phillips stopped mid-sentence, watching him. Henry sat, head down, his slightly-too-long hair falling down over his eyes. Henry's round-framed glasses slid down his sweat-slick nose. He pushed them back up and leaned his forehead on one hand as he opened a notebook and prepared to take notes with the other, barricading himself from her scrutiny.

"Are you Henry?" Mrs. Phillips approached his desk. The rest of the class watched with avid interest.

"Yeah," Henry admitted. He tried to look confidently into her face and saw her eyes widen slightly as she saw his face clearly for the first time.

"Let's go talk in the hall," she suggested.

With the rest of the students' eyes on them, Henry followed Mrs. Phillips out of the room and into the hall. She shut the door as the class began to buzz with gossip. She looked Henry over once more.

"What happened to your eye?"

Henry grimaced nervously. "Looks like someone belted me, huh?" he suggested. "I got up in the night to go to the can," he explained. "Didn't turn on the light. Slipped on my baby brother's toy. I dunno what I hit—the doorknob or the counter or what. Knocked me cold. My ma freaked out this morning. Made me go to the hospital to get it x-rayed. That's how come I'm late."

"Wow." She smiled reassuringly. "I just wanted to be sure. You realize school started two days ago?" She cocked an eyebrow.

Henry's face warmed and a drop of sweat trickled down his back.

"We were on vacation," he explained. "I guess my ma got the start day mixed up. If she doesn't write things down, she gets the days wrong."

"Okay. Go sit down. I'll get you the list of supplies you need and give you the assignments you missed."

"Thanks." Henry breathed a sigh of relief.

They went back into the classroom. Henry slipped into his seat, sweating heavily with everyone's eyes on him. Great way to start school; two days late and with a black eye. Good way to stay unnoticed. At least Mrs. Phillips didn't seem to doubt his story. He waited for his heart to slow back down to normal, glancing around for any of his friends. There were a couple of acquaintances. No one close. But then, he wasn't that close to anyone. He rubbed his palms on his pants and plucked his shirt away from his body to encourage it to dry faster.

Miss Phillips gave him a supply list and assignments that he had missed. She smiled and returned to the front of the room to continue her lecture. Henry read over the assignment and got to work. With any luck, he'd be caught up by the end of the day.

———

He made it through the rest of the morning unscathed. If other teachers noticed his black eye, they didn't say anything about it.

Since it was only a couple of days into the school year, his teachers hadn't covered anything new yet. Just reviewing and warming up their brains for the upcoming semester. He wasn't going to have to do much to catch up.

Henry scanned the cafeteria for familiar faces at lunchtime. It was the first year of high school and there were a lot of unfamiliar people—a lot more faces than there had been in junior high. The room was buzzing with barely controlled chaos. Hearing laughter nearby, Henry focused in on Andrew, a boy he had known since kindergarten. There was an empty seat next to him. Henry moved toward it and looked at Andrew questioningly. Andrew's eyes lit up.

"Henry! Hey man, I haven't seen you around," Andrew enthused. "Thought that maybe you'd moved. Come on, have a seat."

Henry slid into the seat. "Thanks."

Andrew took a bite of his sandwich, looking Henry over.

"Hey, you know you got a shiner?" he asked around a mouthful.

There were giggles from some of the surrounding students. Andrew was kind of a clown. He liked an audience.

"Yeah, I did notice," Henry said dryly.

"You get in a fight or something? I should see the other guy?"

Henry shook his head, carefully peeling back the edges of the plastic wrap of his sandwich. "No… I gotta start putting on my glasses and the light when I get up at night. Stop walking into doors."

Andrew laughed, nodding. "Just how strong are those pop bottles? You blind without them?"

"If it's pitch dark, yeah," Henry agreed. "May as well have my eyes shut. In fact, maybe I'd see better with my eyes shut!"

Andrew giggled. He gestured to the boy seated across from him. "Do you know Tony?"

"No." Henry sketched a salute. "Hi. I'm Henry."

"Henry's a stand-up guy," Andrew declared, "and real handy with homework if you need help. Tony's new this year, just moved into the neighborhood. He's in most of my classes."

Henry nodded, munching on his sandwich. The bread was stale and a bit dry. And there hadn't been nearly enough peanut butter to coat the slices. With just bread and jam, he was going to be starving by the time he got home. But he wasn't using the school lunch program unless he had to. He got teased enough as it was.

"And I guess you know everyone else," Andrew said.

Henry glanced at the others in the immediate vicinity. A few familiar faces from junior high. No one that he was particularly friendly with, but no one who bullied him, either. He got a few nods of greeting.

"Yeah," he agreed. "Hey."

2

———

At the end of the school day, after the dismissal bell, students were hanging around in the hallways, visiting, catching up with old friendships and trying out new ones. Already, there were a few couples lip-locked in front of lockers or in corners, testing out the new freedoms of high school. In junior high, such displays had been immediately broken up by the teachers. In high school, they were ignored. Henry didn't hang around or look for any of his friends. He hurried straight home.

He dropped his books on the kitchen table. Bobby was crying in the bedroom.

"Ma? Ma, are you home?" Henry called, looking around for her.

There was no reply. Henry made his way to his room, where Bobby was standing in his crib screaming. He held onto the bars tightly. The baby's face was red and sweaty. He sounded frantic, like he'd been crying for a long time. When Henry appeared, Bobby immediately reached out his arms, his screams changing in pitch to an urgent *uh-uh-uh!* Henry reached in and picked him up. Bobby clung to him, burying his face in Henry's shirt, his sobs starting to slow. His fingers dug into Henry, sharp

5

nails catching at his skin. He was holding on so tightly that Henry figured if he let him go, he'd hang there without support like a baby monkey. Henry bounced and cuddled him.

"There, you're okay," he murmured. "Henry's here. You're okay."

There were three empty bottles in the crib. Henry collected them with one hand, wedging one under his opposite armpit so he could carry them all without putting Bobby down. He went into the kitchen.

"*Shh, shh,*" he comforted as he jiggled Bobby. He prepared a fresh bottle of formula for Bobby with his free hand and held it in front of him.

"There you go. Why don't you put that in your mouth for a bit?"

Bobby drank the bottle around sniffles and gasps. Henry took him into the bathroom to change his reeking diaper. He gently wiped Bobby's bottom, which started him crying again. His skin was bright red and inflamed, obviously painful to the touch. Henry disposed of the dirty diaper and left Bobby bare-bottomed.

"There. You can play like that while I study and get a snack."

Henry put Bobby down on the kitchen floor and made another jam sandwich for himself. He sat down over his books, eating the sandwich slowly while he read, glancing over at Bobby every few minutes to make sure that he was happy crawling around and kept out of mischief.

The front door opened. Henry looked over his shoulder to see who it was. Clint. A big man, wearing a construction hard-hat, looking unshaven as usual. He was rank with sweat.

"Hi." Henry looked back at his books, uninterested in further interaction.

"Hey, Hank," Clint grunted.

"Don't call me that," Henry objected. "It's Henry."

"Yeah, whatever."

Clint didn't care. He had no intention of showing Henry the respect of calling him by his preferred name.

"You seen my mom?" Henry asked. He leaned back in his chair and rubbed the space between his eyebrows.

"No. She's not home?"

"No."

Obviously. Why would Henry ask if she was there? Clint wasn't the brightest bulb in the box. Clint watched Bobby playing on the floor.

"How come Squirt's got no diaper?"

"He got left in a dirty diaper. It burns his skin. The baby book says the best thing is to let his skin get some air," Henry explained.

"What if he whizzes on the floor?"

"I'll clean it up."

"Okay."

Clint looked around. "I'll see you around, then, Hank."

"You're not staying?"

"Not if Dorry's not home."

He adjusted his hard hat, showing a white band of skin where the hat's front support kept the sun and dirt from darkening his face, and he turned and left. Henry sat for a moment, listening to his retreating footsteps. He shrugged and went back to work.

It was late when the door opened next. Dinner and homework were long since finished. Bobby was back in bed, asleep this time in a clean, dry diaper and onesie, tummy happily full. Henry put down his book and got up off his bed quietly so as not to wake Bobby.

"Ma?"

He walked out to the living room, where she was taking off her shoes and her fall coat. Her face was pale and thin, dark rings under her eyes, her brown hair lank and uncombed over her shoulders. She forced a smile at Henry.

"Hi, Honey. How was your day?"

"You left Bobby alone," Henry accused, ignoring her greeting and question.

"I couldn't take his fussing anymore." Her voice was flat and emotionless. "Don't get on my case."

"You could have called me at school. So I could come home at noon or something."

"I didn't want you to miss any more school. He was okay until you came home."

"You can't leave him alone like that! What if he got out of his crib? Or someone came into the house? You know Social Services would take him away if they knew you left him alone."

"Well," she shook her head slightly, "no one is going to tell them."

"You want him to be taken away?" Henry challenged.

"They'd put him in foster care for a while," she said with a shrug, "and then they'd give him back again."

Henry remembered being in foster care years ago. When she was recovering from a relationship and couldn't 'handle' him. She probably didn't even remember that man's name anymore. But Henry did. He remembered Frank. He remembered a lot more than she thought he did, though neither one of them ever brought it up.

"Bobby's got a real bad rash," Henry told Dorry. "Was he dirty when you left?"

Dorry swept her hair back from her face with both hands in a tired gesture. She went to the fridge and looked through it listlessly, eventually selecting a small juice box of lemonade that sat alone on the top shelf. Henry watched her remove the straw, removed the wrapper from it, and poke it into the top. She took a couple of small sips and put it to the side on the counter, where she probably wouldn't pick it back up again.

"Of course not," she told him. "I made sure he was okay."

"You can't just leave him by himself," Henry repeated. "The baby book—"

"Henry," she interrupted him tiredly, "I don't care what the baby book says. The baby book doesn't have to listen to him cry all the time. I do. You know how he's been the last few days."

"Yeah, 'cause he's been sick. And I was the one taking care of him then, not you. Did you even stay with him at all today? Or did you just put bottles in the crib and leave as soon as I was out of the house?"

"You're not my mom," Dorry snapped, "I'm yours. You don't get to tell me what to do."

Henry exhaled sharply in frustration. He picked his books up from the table, shutting them loudly and putting them into his backpack.

"Is that how you took care of me when I was a baby?"

Dorry looked at him for a moment, her pale brown eyes expressionless. She ruffled his hair. "You turned out okay."

That was as close as she ever got to saying that she loved him. Henry noted that she hadn't answered the question.

———

Henry woke up several times during the night. Not because Bobby was fussing, but just because he was anxious. He would get up and check Bobby's diaper, worried that the rash was going to get worse if Bobby had to sleep the night through in a wet or dirty diaper. He checked Bobby's temperature to make sure that his fever hadn't returned.

When he couldn't think of anything else to check, he just stood there by the crib in the moonlight, looking at Bobby's cherubic face as he slept.

Then Henry climbed back into bed with a sigh and tried to force his mind to slow down and let him return to sleep.

3

———————

Hey, Henry," Andrew sang out, "ain't that the third time today I seen you on the phone?"

Henry started and turned around guiltily. "I don't know, did you see me the other two times?" he quipped, trying to make light of it. The last thing that he needed was for someone to be monitoring how many times he used the phone.

Many of the students had cell phones, but they weren't allowed to use them at school, on threat of having them confiscated. That meant there were long lineups and steep competition for the few payphones, especially during lunchtime or the short breaks between classes. Henry had already been late to a couple of classes and used the phone when he had been excused to use the restroom.

Andrew laughed. "Yeah, man. What's up, you got girl problems?"

Henry gave him a significant look and turned his back on Andrew again, facing the phone and waiting worriedly for an answer.

"You wanna give me some privacy?" he suggested, hoping that Andrew would just go with the idea that Henry was trying to connect up with some girl and leave him alone.

The answering machine picked up. Henry frowned, waving Andrew off. The boy finally backed off, laughing. Henry cupped his hand around the receiver so that no one would overhear him.

"Mom, it's me," he said urgently. "Pick up if you're home."

After a moment, there was a click. Henry sighed with relief.

"What's up?" It was Clint's rough, impatient voice.

"Oh, hi. Mom's not there?"

"No."

"Is Bobby there? Do you want me to come home?" Henry suggested worriedly.

"He's fine. Dorry decided to take him to that moms and tots thing. And he'll be tired and have a nap when she gets back."

Henry breathed out. "Good. Are you gonna be there after school?"

"More than likely," Clint growled. "So?"

"If you're both there, maybe I'll go to the mall for a bit after school. You can have some time to yourselves."

Clint grunted. "Sure. Just don't stay out too long. She'll get worried."

"No," Henry agreed. "Just an hour or something. I won't be long."

Clint hung up. Henry replaced the receiver slowly. He felt a rush of relief. He could finally relax and concentrate on his classes. Bobby was okay. There was nothing for him to worry about. He moved away from the phone to let the next person make their call.

———

Henry wandered through the mall, happy to relax and not have any responsibilities for a few minutes.

A lot of the stores had signs up. *Schoolbags and knapsacks to be left at the front of the store.* They were afraid of kids shoplifting.

Henry left his knapsack at the front of the electronics store. If someone really wanted to shoplift, they wouldn't need a knapsack to do it. The clerks couldn't watch everyone if the store was busy. They disregarded Henry as a shoplifter as soon as he walked in the door. He didn't look like trouble. A nice kid. A geek with glasses. None of the clerks were watching him. He could pocket a pack of batteries or anything that wasn't tied down that would fit in his pocket. Henry picked up the batteries and weighed them in his hand.

All he would have to do was to slip them into his pocket.

———

Henry found himself picking up his knapsack at the front of the store with the weight of the batteries in his pocket.

His heart was racing and he felt lightheaded, like he was going to pass out. He turned around to tell the clerk how bad their security was and prove to them how easy it was to shoplift. But that would be stupid. They could put him in jail for what he had just done. He considered going back into the store and putting the batteries back. But that would be risky. Going back in would be suspicious. Better to just walk away.

On the way home, he realized he was grinning. It had been so easy to lift the batteries! He had done it right under their noses, without anybody suspecting a thing. And he felt—what? Powerful. Superior. Exhilarated. And just a little bit guilty. He was still breathless with excitement. It was an odd feeling. He had foolishly followed a compulsion and had gotten away with it. He received no punishment, no consequence. And he was one pack of batteries richer for it.

Before he got home, he put the batteries in his knapsack. No point letting his mom find them in his pocket if she decided to do laundry.

———

"That you, Henry?" Dorry called when he opened the front door.

"Hi, ma," Henry greeted, sticking his head around the corner on his way to the kitchen.

"You're late getting home."

Henry stopped. He frowned and went into the living room where his mom and Clint were sitting on the couch watching TV. Clint was in his undershirt, one arm around Dorry. She had her head nestled in his shoulder and her legs stretched across his lap.

"I told Clint," Henry pointed out uncertainly.

Dorry looked up at Clint for verification. He set down his beer on the side table, nodding, wiping his mouth with the back of his hand.

"Yeah," Clint confirmed. "He called while you were out with Squirt."

"You didn't tell me!"

"You weren't worried." Clint scratched his bristly chin, looking back at the TV.

Dorry fished for an explanation, not wanting to sound like she hadn't cared that Henry hadn't come straight home. "I didn't realize how late it was until I heard you come in."

Henry shrugged. He picked Bobby up from where he was playing on the rug and bounced him, making Bobby crow loudly, all smiles.

"Hey, buddy! How was your day?" he said in his high baby-talk voice. "You went out with mama? Had a fun day?" He tickled Bobby.

"He loves that playgroup," Dorry observed. "Maybe I'll take him again next week."

"Good," Henry approved. It was good for her to have somewhere to take him. Somewhere that she could meet with other adults, good examples, and socialize with them. "I'll go study in my room," he offered, "take him along with me."

"Thanks, bud," Dorry said, smiling gently. "You're a good kid."

As he retreated from the room, Dorry put her arms around Clint's neck, pulling him close for a kiss. Henry felt his face growing hot. He grabbed a banana from the kitchen counter and hurried down the hall. He closed his door to shut out their low murmurs.

4

───────

Bobby had been fussing for a while before Henry finally managed to fully rouse himself from sleep. He stumbled to his feet, rubbing his sticky, sleepy eyes with his palms. He turned on the night-light and patted Bobby soothingly on the back.

"What's the matter, Bobby? You hungry?" he questioned softly. Even in the dim light, he could see how red the baby's cheeks were. "You teething, bud?"

Henry rubbed Bobby's back in slow circles, seeing if he would settle. Bobby continued to sob and fuss. Henry left him in the crib and shuffled out to the kitchen. He blearily prepared a bottle.

"Can't you shut that kid up?" Clint demanded, stalking into the kitchen.

"He's teething," Henry said tersely, struggling to screw the top onto the bottle. But it kept getting cross-threaded and he couldn't get it on straight.

"I said to shut him up!" Clint repeated.

"I'm trying!"

Clint aimed a kick at the back of Henry's knees. Henry was still half asleep, and both knees buckled. The bottle went flying, a pool of milk spreading across the floor. Henry swore, staggering to his feet.

"What did you do that for?" he protested. He knew he'd made a mistake the minute the words left his mouth and threw up his hand to protect himself. "I'm sorry, I'm sorry! I didn't mean—"

Clint raised his hand, eyes calculating. He backhanded Henry powerfully across the cheek, throwing him to the floor.

"Don't you *ever* back-talk me!"

Henry's mother came into the kitchen, pulling her tatty housecoat shut across her thin body. She tied it messily.

"Clint, leave him alone. Go back to bed," she coaxed.

"I have to sleep," Clint griped, "can't have that baby keeping me awake at all hours." He started walking back toward the bedroom. "You'd better make sure he cleans up in there."

"He will," Dorry assured him. "Go on."

Clint shut the bedroom door. Dorry reached down and helped Henry to his feet. "Come on, sweetie," she encouraged.

Henry got up, holding his throbbing face. "I'm gonna be bruised for school," he said, his throat constricted and hot tears overflowing his eyes. He sniffled, silent sobs shaking his belly. He couldn't miss more school so soon.

"It'll be okay," Dorry said soothingly. "I'll get you some ice."

"I gotta get Bobby his milk and clean up," Henry's voice shook.

"I'll clean up. You take your brother his bottle. I'll bring you ice when you're done."

His breathing still shaky, Henry got a new bottle for Bobby, who was now wailing full force in the bedroom.

Henry picked Bobby up and lay down with him on the bed to feed him. Bobby fussed a bit, then settled down to take the bottle and soon fell back asleep. Henry rested quietly, cuddled up with Bobby, waiting for his mother to bring the ice. Dorry eventually came in and handed him a frozen gel pack. She sat on the edge of the bed and examined his cheek.

"I don't think it's too bad," she told him. "If anyone notices, just say you fell down."

"Yeah, right," Henry snapped. "I tripped and fell on my face. Social Services would be here before I got out of school."

"Maybe it won't even show."

"It'll show. Why'd he have to do that?" Henry whined.

"You know better than to talk back to Clint."

"I said I was sorry. I didn't *mean* to; he just startled me. I didn't have time to think."

"He's like that when his sleep gets interrupted. It's not really his fault." Dorry ran her fingers through her sleep-tangled hair. "I gotta get back to bed. You get some sleep. Everybody will feel better in the morning."

5

Henry adjusted his glasses, nudging them slightly so they didn't press against his bruised cheek. He took a deep breath and picked up his books. Keeping his face turned away from Mrs. Phillips, who was his homeroom teacher as well as his English Language Arts teacher, he slipped into his desk. With his elbow on his desk, he leaned on his hand, covering the bruise casually.

Mrs. Phillips came in and called the class to order to make the morning announcements. She read them out over the low buzz of conversations. The class change bell rang. Henry stayed where he was while some of the other students left for classes in other rooms. Once the class was assembled, Mrs. Phillips called for their summer essays. They passed their assignments forward to the front desks. The class quieted abruptly, and Henry looked up to see what was going on. Mrs. Phillips was gazing at Henry, her eyebrows drawn down in a frown. When his gaze met hers, Mrs. Phillips quirked her mouth in half smile.

"Forget to turn the light on again?" she asked in a low voice.

Henry started to sweat, putting his hand back up to touch the bruise. His mind raced. "I was messing around with my

18

friend's skateboard," he explained, mouth dry. "I sorta hit a tree."

He looked down, his face burning as he knew he flushed bright pink. Mrs. Phillips approached his desk and put her hand on his shoulder as she took a long, close look at his bruised cheek. Finally, she shook her head and laughed. "You have to be more careful, Henry."

"I know. I feel so stupid; I'm always such a klutz." Henry wiped sweat from his forehead.

"Were you wearing a helmet and pads?"

Henry shook his head. "Don't I look enough like a geek with these glasses?"

Mrs. Phillips smiled. "Oh, you don't look like a geek. Just like a kid with glasses."

"Around here, that's what you call a geek," Henry explained.

Mrs. Phillips laughed appreciatively. There were a few giggles from the students close enough to have overheard the conversation. Mrs. Phillips returned to the front to continue the class. Henry pulled his shirt away from his armpits, breathing deeply.

The hallways were crowded and noisy. Henry looked around for any friends. He saw Tony, Andrew's new friend, talking with some others in the hall. He walked up and joined them. The boys nodded or grinned and continued their conversation. James, one of the boys in Henry's homeroom, was holding a skateboard. He put it down and kicked it over to Henry.

"Hey, Henry. I hear you got some pretty good moves. Let's see some tricks."

Henry felt his ears get hot. The others stopped talking and looked at him for his reaction. Henry kicked the skateboard back with his toe.

"You don't wanna see my moves," he countered, "and anyway, there ain't any trees to run into here!"

The boys laughed. One of them gestured to Henry. "Is that what happened to your face?"

"Yeah," Henry chuckled, shaking his head. "Close encounter with a tree. You'd think with these big feet, I'd have some kind of balance."

He showed off his kicks. They all started comparing shoe sizes to see who had the biggest feet. It was no surprise that Lorne, a halfback who'd been held back twice, had the biggest shoe size. But Henry's were right up there.

"Man, you do have big feet for a little guy," Lorne admitted, surprised.

Henry nodded proudly, grinning. "I even have to get new shoes. These ones are pinching."

"That means you're gonna be tall, you know," James pointed out.

"That, or short with really big feet," Andrew interjected with a laugh.

"What about your folks. How tall are they?" Lorne questioned.

Henry considered the question. "Ma's pretty tall for a girl," he mused. "I dunno about my dad; she's never said."

"Is it true what they say?" Tony questioned. "You know, about guys with big feet…"

Henry had just been relaxing and getting to enjoy the conversation, but his face got hot again and he looked away from the group, rubbing his forehead to hide his flushed face from them. There were whoops of laughter from the group. He joined in the laughter half-heartedly and looked for a way to change the subject or escape from the group.

6

It was getting late in the afternoon, and Henry knew that he should be heading home, but he was at the mall, browsing through shoes at the department store. He really did need new ones, as he'd told Lorne. But every time Henry looked at a price tag, he winced. They were so expensive. He knew what Dorry would say if he told her he had outgrown his shoes again already. She always complained about much it cost to take care of him. And the shoes that he liked were over a hundred bucks. She would never even consider them. He'd end up with a pair of ten-dollar tennis shoes.

Even though he knew that there was no way he could afford them, Henry tried on a pair of the expensive runners and walked up the aisle. They were so comfortable. It was nice not to have shoes that squeezed and pinched his toes. They were a popular brand. Lots of the guys had them. Henry had never gone for the most stylish brands or passing fads, but those shoes… he really liked them. He could picture himself walking to school in them. Hanging out with the other guys in them. They were really nice.

He snapped the plastic string holding the two shoes together so that he could walk with his full stride and get a better feel for them. The price tags came off in his hand and he stuffed them into his pocket temporarily. Henry walked around the shoe department for a few minutes, thinking about ways to raise the money to get shoes like this.

Dorry wouldn't let him get a job delivering newspapers or flyers. She needed him to look after Bobby and was insistent that he get enough sleep himself. Henry had a sneaking suspicion that she would turn down any sort of job that he suggested. It would cut into his babysitting time or schoolwork. And for him to get a job just to get an expensive pair of shoes… she'd think that was stupid.

He thought back to the batteries. It had been incredibly easy to just walk out of the store with them. As long as he looked honest and confident, like he had nothing to hide, no one would look at him twice. Who'd be looking at his shoes? Henry stood there for a long time, thinking about it.

When he finally moved, he kicked his old shoes underneath a shelf and walked toward the store entrance. But he didn't walk straight out. He selected a chocolate bar that he had enough change to buy and went through the checkout line. He opened it as he walked to the doors. The greeter at the exit stopped him.

"You have the receipt for that?" she demanded, gesturing at the chocolate bar.

Henry displayed it. She looked Henry over suspiciously.

"You mind showing me what's in your bag?"

Henry shrugged and put his backpack down on the floor in front of his feet, where she could open it. Good thing he hadn't put his old shoes in it. She would have immediately looked at the new shoes on his feet and known what was going on. The woman took a brief look through Henry's schoolbooks and supplies.

"Okay. Sorry. Go ahead," she told him.

Henry picked up his backpack and walked out of the store.

———

Henry stopped a block away and took a deep breath to calm himself. Had he looked suspicious? Was that why she had stopped him? Or was it just a random thing? He was sweating heavily, his heart pounded hard, and he was out of breath. He had that same feeling of exhilaration he had when he took the batteries. Maybe even more so. It was the second time he hadn't gotten caught. The batteries were only a couple of bucks, but the shoes were worth more than anything he owned. The shoes were cool.

Henry laughed out loud with the relief of getting away with it. He picked up his bag again and headed for home at a quick clip, humming to himself.

———

He arrived home to an empty house. The car was not parked in front of the house. There was no moms and tots program on a Thursday, so he wasn't sure where Dorry had gone, but he was glad that she had at least taken Bobby with her.

After working through his homework, Henry got up to look for something to eat. The fridge was practically empty. He wasn't sure what he was going to eat. They at least had the formula that some social program had paid for so Bobby wouldn't starve, but Henry was getting pretty hungry. There was nothing for sandwiches the next day, so he might have to break down and use the school lunch program after all. There was a lump in his stomach at the thought that had nothing to do with hunger.

The front door opened and Henry closed the fridge door. Dorry came in, Bobby on her hip and a shopping bag in the opposite hand.

"Oh, hi honey. How was school?"

Henry shrugged. "Okay. You took Bobby out with you?"

"Just to pick up some beer, yeah."

He looked down at the contents of her shopping bag and saw that was all that she had—a case of beer and nothing else.

"Did you put him in his car seat?" he questioned.

"I can never do that thing up. He's getting too big for it, anyway."

Henry nodded. "We need to get the next size up."

"They're so expensive. He's okay just down to the store."

Henry wasn't even sure how she would transport him to the store without the car seat. Strap him in using the seat belt? Just put him on the floor of the car? He was horrified, thinking of what could happen.

"If you were in an accident—" he started sharply.

"I'm careful."

"Someone else could hit you."

"No one hit me, Henry. Quit fussing."

Her dismissive tone closed the conversation. She didn't want to hear any more arguments from him. Henry took the beer from her bag and put it into the fridge with a clang.

"We need groceries," he told her flatly.

Dorry took out her wallet. She swept her lanky hair aside from her face and over her shoulder. She pulled a few bills out of the wallet and handed them to Henry.

"Take Bobby with you."

Henry took him from her. The baby burbled happily, slapping his hand on Henry's arm and face. His diaper clearly needed to be changed.

"Anything you want?" he asked Dorry.

"Orange juice."

Henry nodded. "Okay."

"The fresh, not the frozen."

"I know, Ma."

Henry got the stroller out of the closet with one hand and pushed it open. He took Bobby to the bathroom to change him before leaving. Henry talked animatedly to Bobby, keeping him entertained and distracted. "Did you go out in the car with

Mama? You want to go to the grocery store now? Come on, let's go get some milk, and juice, and bread. Maybe some macaroni too, huh?"

He made sure there were more diapers in the diaper bag and prepared a bottle for Bobby. He loaded everything into the stroller and walked to the grocery store. Henry counted the money Dorry had given him and studied prices as he wound through the aisles to see how far he could stretch the meager amount.

7

———————

Henry was walking back from the store, the groceries in the basket under the stroller. Bobby was squirming around, babbling, and waving his hands at the shivering leaves of the trees. Henry talked to him, enjoying seeing him happy. The air was warm but breezy, keeping Henry from getting too hot. The birds were chirping. A man mowed his lawn, the noise of the lawn mowing droning sleepily.

Henry frowned, looking at the lawnmower man again. He was almost sure… the man was a little heavier, starting to gray a little. But Henry was sure it was him.

"Frank?" he called tentatively, not quite believing it.

The man turned the mower off and looked across the yard at Henry, frowning.

"Did you call me, kid?"

"You are Frank, aren't you?" Henry questioned. His hands were suddenly slippery on the handle of the stroller. He had never expected to see Frank again, after all of these years. Frank was a distant memory.

"Yeah. Do I know you?" Frank questioned. He took a couple of steps toward Henry.

"Henry Thomas," Henry said. "Do you remember…?"

"Henry?" Frank said in disbelief. "What are you doing here?"

"I live just down the block," Henry gestured in the general direction.

Frank frowned, shaking his head. He scratched his head. His hair had thinned over the years too. Henry was surprised that he looked so much older. "It's been... well, a lot of years."

"Nine, I think," Henry said, quickly subtracting the years.

"Huh. I just moved here over the summer."

Neither of them spoke for a few moments. Henry didn't know what to say or how to act. He and Frank had been really close when Frank had been seeing his mom. Henry had never loved anyone more. Maybe not even his mom. He had been devastated when Frank and Dorry had broken up. Frank was the only man who'd ever been like a father to Henry.

He wanted to throw his arms around Frank, to ask him how he could have stayed away for so long. He wanted to feel safe in Frank's arms again. But guys Henry's age didn't do that. Henry just stood there, trying to figure out what to say.

"So, is this your brother?" Frank questioned finally, his eyes turning to Bobby. "One of a long line?" he suggested.

"No, just me and him," Henry said with a short laugh.

"I always thought Dorry would have a whole houseful of kids," Frank said, smiling, his eyes reminiscent.

"No. She doesn't like kids," Henry said flatly.

"She used to. I wonder what made her change her mind."

Henry thought back to that time. She had been happy when Frank was around. They had been a real family. Having fun times together, going out, lots of hugs and kisses. After they broke up, Dorry went into a deep depression. That was when Henry had been put into foster care. Things had never been the same after that. Dorry never smiled much when Henry returned. He tried to make her happy, but he couldn't replace Frank.

"Things weren't really the same after you left," Henry told Frank, shrugging and looking away.

Frank looked saddened. He stared down at the baby. They both looked down at Bobby, too hurt to look each other in the eye.

"How much do you remember about when me and your mom were together?" Frank asked awkwardly.

"I remember," Henry asserted. He might have been young at the time, but he remembered everything that Frank had been to them.

Frank touched Henry's chin, lifting his face so that they were eye to eye. Frank stared into Henry's eyes for a disconcertingly long time. Henry frowned, wondering why Frank was being so intense. He was overwhelmed with Frank being so close to him. That familiar face. Those eyes. Even the smell of him brought back so many memories. Frank looked so sad and worried. Henry gave in to impulse and threw his arms around Frank.

"I missed you. I never thought I'd see you again," he murmured.

For a moment, Frank stood there, stiff and rigid, shocked by the contact. Then he pulled Henry's head against his chest and kissed him warmly on the top of his head.

"I missed you too, sport," he said hoarsely.

Henry walked in the door. He took a deep breath and let it out again. He got Bobby out of the stroller and put him on the floor to play.

"You took a while at the grocery store," Dorry observed. "You run into problems?"

"No."

Henry opened his mouth to tell her about Frank, then closed it, reconsidering. She had split up with Frank, even knowing how close Henry was to him. She hadn't let Frank come over to visit or let Henry continue to go on outings with him. She had erased Frank from their lives, knowing how it would hurt Henry. She'd been more worried about whatever they'd broken up over than about her own son's feelings.

"It was just busy today," Henry told her. "Long lineups."

Henry started to unpack the groceries and put them away. His stomach was tense. He felt guilty about lying to her.

"Do you want me to make you some supper?" he offered. Maybe doing something nice for her would make him feel better about the lie.

"Oh, I'm not hungry, honey. Really. You go ahead and make something for yourself."

She turned away from him to leave the room.

"You don't eat enough, Ma," Henry objected. "You're getting too skinny."

Dorry laughed and patted her flat stomach.

"Someone once said you can never be too rich or too skinny."

"Someone never heard of malnutrition or anorexia," Henry shot back. She went into the living room to watch TV, and Henry took care of his and Bobby's supper.

8

———————

Henry sat in math class the next day, thinking about Frank. He couldn't understand Frank's awkwardness and reticence. It had been a long time since they saw each other, but Henry and Frank had always gotten along well. Whatever had happened to split them up had been between Frank and Dorry.

It was that long, piercing stare that was so disconcerting. Like he was trying to look into Henry's heart, to read his memories. Why wouldn't Henry remember him? It had been a lot of years ago, but how could Henry forget all the good times they'd had together?

Frank had seemed so awkward and worried. Like he was afraid of even talking to Henry. Henry decided to go see him again after school, once he had checked on Bobby.

Funny what Frank had said about Dorry wanting a lot of kids. She couldn't handle kids crying and getting underfoot. For a long time after Frank had left, Henry didn't think she even liked him anymore. Maybe Henry had reminded her of Frank too much. The way little kids chatter, Henry had probably asked after Frank constantly after he had disappeared. Funny though, Henry couldn't remember any of their conversations after Frank had left. He clearly remembered the many outings with Frank and the time they'd spent together. But the period between Frank leaving and the year or two after that was fuzzy and muddled.

When Dorry had accidentally gotten pregnant with Bobby, she and Clint had nearly broken up. They had long, loud, emotional arguments about the pregnancy. Dorry wanted an abortion. Clint was dead set against it. That was when Clint had turned to Henry, asking him to make sure she took good care of herself while pregnant. He had bought a baby care book and gave it to Henry to read. His mom eventually accepted the idea of continuing the pregnancy and stayed pretty much confined to bed. When Bobby was born, responsibility was handed over to Clint and Henry. But Clint was a bear if wakened in the night; so much so that Henry feared for the baby's safety and moved the crib into his own room. During the day, Clint worked, so it fell to Henry to juggle school and baby care, relying on Dorry to do little more than give Bobby an occasional bottle.

Someone poked Henry in the back, and he jolted and looked around. The class was silent, everyone looking at him. Mr. Abrams looked at him expectantly, obviously having asked him a question. Henry scanned the board and looked down at his books.

"What?"

A few classmates giggled.

"Would you like to join us on this planet?" the teacher said sarcastically.

"Sorry," Henry apologized, "I was just… distracted. Sorry."

"Did you do your homework last night?"

"Yes."

"We're on 5(c). You want to walk us through it?"

"Uh, sure."

Henry read through the question, ears burning, and then read through his answer, squirming uncomfortably in his seat.

———

Henry knew he had to see Frank again. Maybe he shouldn't, but he really needed to see him again, visit with him. He went to Frank's house after school. Another man answered the door. This was unexpected. Henry stood there, uncertain what to say.

"Well, what do you want?" the stranger questioned impatiently.

"Um—sorry… I was looking for Frank?"

"Hang on." The man withdrew and shouted, "Frank, you got a visitor."

He walked away without another word. Henry stood at the door waiting. Frank came down the stairs and saw him.

"Oh… it's you. What do you want, Henry?" he demanded.

"I… I just wanted to visit you," Henry said, his voice small and faint in his own ears.

"Well, I really don't know…" Frank scratched the back of his neck and looked around.

Henry tried to mask his disappointment and figure out why Frank didn't want to see him again.

"Are you busy?" he questioned. "I could come back later…"

"No, it's not that."

"What, then?" Henry demanded, his voice cracking. "I thought you said you missed me too."

Frank nodded. "Yeah, I do," he looked reminiscent, despite his previous tone. "We had some good times together, didn't we?" he murmured.

Henry nodded eagerly. "We used to do all kinds of things—going to the zoo, or the park, or the mall. I know I'm not a little kid anymore. We're not gonna do any of that kind of stuff. But I want to… visit with you. Be with you again."

Frank sighed. "Well, you'd better come in off the doorstep anyways," he conceded finally, stepping back and motioning Henry to enter.

Henry stepped in and looked around. The room was sort of

dim and disorderly, with a greasy food smell in the air. It was sparsely furnished and felt empty.

"So the other guy, you're roommates?" Henry questioned.

"Well, housemates, yeah. It's a—a few of us share the rent. We don't have that much to do with each other. Other than living in the same house."

Henry nodded. They both looked around for somewhere to sit. It was not an inviting room.

"Why don't you come in the kitchen, and we'll have some lemonade or something," Frank suggested.

The kitchen was brighter and looked relatively unused, despite the smell of the place. Henry supposed that a group of carefree bachelors probably didn't do a lot of cooking. They probably ate mostly takeout and frozen dinners.

Frank rummaged around in the fridge and came up with some pale-colored punch. "I don't know what kind it is. Cherry or something," he said apologetically.

Henry thought he was probably lucky the bachelors had anything other than beer.

"That's okay."

Frank opened the freezer to find ice cubes.

"Do you remember we used to make popsicles together?" Henry said suddenly, the memory jumping to the front of his mind, "out of juice, or yogurt, or pudding? I remember that!"

"Sure, we made some pretty decent stuff, too. You still like to mess around in the kitchen?" Frank questioned, putting a glass on the table in front of Henry. He sat down across the table.

"I do most of the cooking," Henry said.

"What's your mom do? Work?"

Henry was embarrassed to have Frank ask after Dorry like that. Casually, like he'd never been close to her.

"Ma doesn't handle stress so well… Sometimes she'll work at something for a few weeks. Then," he shrugged, "she either gets fired or quits. And she hasn't done much since Bobby was born."

"Well, a baby takes up a lot of time. Did she get married, then? She's got someone to look after her?"

"No… we have Clint. He's been around for a couple of years. He helps out a bit with the bills. And Ma gets welfare checks and disability."

"Disability?" Frank repeated.

Henry shrugged and looked down. He didn't explain.

"I always figured to marry your mom. I've never really met anyone I got along with like her," Frank said.

"Then why did you guys break up?"

They looked at each other for a moment, each aware of the raw emotion in the other's eyes. Neither could voice their innermost feelings.

"I don't think we should talk about it," Frank said finally.

"Yeah," Henry agreed.

He knew it wasn't a fair question to ask. He'd heard plenty of times how breakups and divorces were never just one person's fault. About how some relationships just weren't meant to be. It wasn't fair to ask why. It wasn't Frank's fault that they had broken up. It had been Dorry. She was the one who was so bitter and wouldn't have anything to do with him again.

9

Henry went to Frank's house a lot over the fall. Sometimes he'd go by himself, and sometimes he'd take Bobby. They would sit in the kitchen or out in the backyard talking. Frank let down his guard and seemed more natural as time went on. But a few times, Henry was sure that there was something Frank was not telling him.

One time, Henry had taken Bobby with him and Frank asked to hold him.

"Yeah, sure," Henry said, and took Bobby out of the stroller.

Frank sat Bobby in his lap and bounced him.

"He's a pretty good baby?" he asked, smiling, looking like this was how it was supposed to be, a father figure yet again, happy to be holding a child.

"Yeah," Henry agreed. "I worry about him, though. About if we're raising him right. Taking good enough care of him."

"He seems happy and healthy," Frank said, looking at Bobby's face, still bouncing him.

"Yeah. But ma doesn't really look after him, and I just go by the book..." Henry trailed off.

Frank suddenly looked down at Bobby with a different expression on his face.

"You'd better take him back," he said hurriedly, picking Bobby up and handing him over.

"Is he wet?" Henry questioned, thinking he recognized that look. Bobby's diaper must have leaked on Frank's pants.

"No. I just remembered I have to be somewhere," Frank said hurriedly, standing up and moving away sideways, crablike. "We'll have to do this some other time."

Frank disappeared into the house. Henry stood there with Bobby, staring after him, trying to figure out what had just happened.

———

Henry got the diaper bag together and got Bobby into the stroller. Dorry looked up from the TV and rubbed her temples tiredly. "Where are you going?"

"Taking Bobby to the doctor," Henry told her patiently. She should have known already. Not only was it written on the calendar, but he'd told her not half an hour ago.

"He's not sick, though," she protested.

"No. It's just a 'well-baby' check-up."

"If he's not sick, why does he need a check-up?"

"Just to make sure he's growing and developing like he is supposed to," Henry explained. Hadn't she taken Henry to doctor's appointments when he was a baby? Had she just forgotten how it worked or had she not bothered when he was a baby?

Dorry shook her head, then shrugged. "I don't know why he needs one, but... whatever."

Henry put a bottle of formula into the diaper bag and handed Bobby a rattly teething toy. They waited for a while at the doctor's office. Bobby was doing pretty well, not making a lot of noise. Henry was glad that he wasn't crawling around yet. The other kids were coughing and slobbering over the doctor's toys. Henry read the public health posters on the wall and picked up a couple of pamphlets on nutrition and development, tucking them into the diaper bag.

The doctor asked questions while he weighed and measured Bobby and checked his eyes and ears, listened to his chest and back with his stethoscope, and so on. He sat down and wrote some notes on the file. He looked up at Henry, crossing one leg across his other knee.

"So, tell me something, Henry," he said.

Henry shifted uneasily. "Yeah?"

"Are you taking care of this baby by yourself?'

Henry's heart thumped and his breathing felt strangled. He looked into the doctor's eyes, but they were not accusatory, only inquiring.

"Is there something wrong with him?" Henry stalled.

"No, no. Very healthy, happy, strong boy. Developmentally on par," the doctor assured him.

"Then why do you think I'm taking care of him alone?"

"We don't generally see babies in here with kids your age. Unless they're teenage moms. Now, confidentially, are you?"

Henry tried to figure out what to tell him. The doctor seemed trustworthy. His face was sympathetic. The doctor smiled encouragingly.

"My mom looks after him while I'm at school," Henry said slowly. "The rest of the time..." he hesitated, "Yeah, mostly."

"Are you managing okay? There are places you can go for help. Community resources."

Henry licked his dry lips. "People that won't tell Social Services that Bobby's neglected or something?"

"I can't promise that, but I don't think you'll run into problems. You're doing a good job and you don't need to be penalized for getting some extra help if you need it."

Henry nodded. "Now and then, I wish there was someone I could trust to look after him when I've got somewhere else I have to be," he admitted.

"I'll get you a list. There are some good programs that I think could help you."

"Okay, thanks."

10

———

Henry was sitting in the kitchen with Frank, visiting and having a lemonade. Bobby was playing happily on the floor. Frank went to the fridge to refill their drinks. They were having a good visit. Frank was loose and relaxed, not uptight like he was some days.

The doorbell rang and there were low voices when it was answered. Henry looked down at Bobby to make sure that he was still happy. When he looked back up at Frank, two uniformed police officers came through the kitchen doorway.

"Frank Wilson?" one of them snapped out.

Frank turned slowly away from the fridge, toward them.

"Yes," he said, sounding defeated.

"You're under arrest. Parole violation."

Frank allowed himself to be frisked and cuffed. Henry stood there frozen, his mouth hanging open. The first cop took Frank out of the room. The other officer addressed Henry.

"Are you okay, kid?" he questioned with concern.

"Yeah, sure," Henry said blankly.

"Let's get you home," he said. He nodded to Bobby. "Is he with you?"

"Yes."

The cop scooped Bobby up and took Henry firmly by the arm, tugging him.

"Come on, son," he encouraged.

"What's going on?" Henry questioned, not comprehending. It was happening so fast. He couldn't get his brain to process it properly

"Come on. We'll explain when we get you somewhere safe."

Henry looked around the kitchen. It *was* a safe place. It was a place where he felt safe and comfortable. What did the cop mean?

There were several police cars in front of the house. They were putting Frank into the back of one of them. The cop holding Henry's arm walked him over to another of the waiting squad cars. There was a baby seat in it for Bobby and Henry buckled him in automatically, his fingers moving on their own will, disengaged from his brain.

"Where do you live?" the cop questioned.

Henry gave his address.

"Nice and close," the man commented.

He pulled out without a word and drove in silence. He then escorted Henry to the door, Bobby in Henry's arms. Dorry answered the bell.

"Henry? What's going on?" she demanded, looking at Henry with wide, worried eyes.

"Ma'am, I'm Officer Bryant," the police officer said, his voice a little louder and sterner than necessary. "Can we come in?"

Dorry shrugged, stepping back. "Yeah, sure. Is Henry in trouble? What did he do?"

They all went into the living room. Dorry made an effort to pick things up and make it look more presentable.

"Henry?" she prompted.

Henry just looked at her blankly, unable to explain.

"Henry's not in trouble, ma'am," Bryant answered, "but he

could have been hurt. We picked him up at the home of a convicted pedophile."

"What was he doing there?" Dorry's face flushed dark. She turned to Henry. "Henry? What are you doing hanging around a place like that?"

Henry opened his mouth to defend himself and couldn't get the words out. His brain was whirling. Convicted pedophile? Did Bryant mean that one of the men at Frank's house was a pedophile? Not Frank himself; Henry knew that Frank wasn't like that. He was a normal guy. Better than normal, he was a friendly, loving, fatherly figure. He was Frank.

"The man was on parole," Bryant explained, "and we got a tip that he had been seen in the company of children, which of course is a parole violation. So he's on his way back to jail." Bryant looked at Henry and kept his voice low and even, like if he spoke gently, Henry wouldn't hear him. "I don't know if anything happened between them. I'd like to know whether we should be laying new charges."

Dorry looked panic-stricken. Her eyes sought Henry's wide and scared. "Honey? Did he hurt you? Did he touch you?"

Henry tried to find his voice. He had to explain. Then she would understand, and not look so scared. "Ma—Ma, it was Frank. *Our* Frank."

The flushed color drained from Dorry's cheeks. "If he's done anything else to hurt you, I'll kill him with my bare hands!" she said vehemently.

Henry stared at her, floored. Her reaction was totally unexpected. *Hurt him?* Frank would never hurt him!

"You know this low-life?" Bryant asked.

"I used to live with him," Dorry sighed, "years ago. And if I'd known he was back in the neighborhood again, I'd'a' seen him run out of town!" Her voice was bitter, vicious. Henry couldn't remember ever hearing her talk like that before.

"Frank didn't do anything," Henry told her, shaking his head. "We just—"

"How could you start seeing him behind my back like that?" Dorry demanded, turning on Henry. He found himself taking a quick step back from her, holding his hands up protectively. "How could you do something like that?"

"I didn't do anything behind your back," Henry protested.

"I thought you had a girlfriend you were sneaking off with. If you weren't trying to keep it from me, why didn't you tell me he was living close by?"

"I didn't think you'd want to know," Henry said defensively, "because you guys broke up."

"And why do you think I broke up with him?"

"I don't remember," Henry said, eyes stinging. He shook his head and shrugged helplessly.

Dorry looked at him in disbelief. "You don't remember."

"No."

"Good grief, Henry!" her voice was scathing. "How could you not remember? You remember everything!"

Henry's eyes burned and there was a hard, hot lump in his throat, but he tried to keep a brave face for the cop. "I don't remember, Mama. All I remember is him going away, and being upset about it."

"We broke up because of you. Because I caught him… doing things he shouldn't." Her final words were almost a whisper. She flushed again, with shame this time instead of anger.

"Frank would never hurt me!" Henry's voice cracked. "Why would you say that?"

"Because he did," Dorry said flatly. "I know you think he was the greatest guy in the world, but he wasn't. He was just really good at pretending. I thought he'd be out of our lives when I kicked him out. Then there was a big to-do in the papers a couple of years later when he was caught doing it again, to another kid, and I testified and helped put him away." Her voice rose until she was nearly shouting, "Then he has the nerve to come back to this neighborhood and mess with you again!"

"He didn't do anything!" Henry yelled back, appalled.

"That's what you said the first time, too. When I saw with my own eyes! They said I should get you counseling, but I thought it was best to just let you forget and move on. Maybe if I'd got you counseling, you wouldn't have let this happen again."

"Do you want to lay charges?" Bryant questioned gently, reminding them he was still there.

Henry's mom rolled her eyes and she let out her breath in a long, angry exhalation. "He won't tell us what happened. I'll have to take him to the doctor and see what they can tell. Where do I take him for that?"

"They can do a forensic kit in the emergency room," Bryant advised, "and someone from the Crisis Center can talk to him. If you like, I can take you there now. You don't want to destroy evidence by waiting."

"I can't believe this is happening again," Dorry grumbled. "Yeah, I guess we'd better go."

"Ma, I don't want doctors poking around there," Henry's face was hot and sweat starting under his armpits. "That's— that's embarrassing."

"Well, you should have worried about that before you got involved with a—with Frank again."

"I swear, all we ever did was talk!"

She shook her head at him and raised her hands palms-up. "You lied to me about it with a straight face all those years ago. I can't let him get away with it again," she said flatly.

Bryant drove them to the hospital and talked to the staff for them.

11

———————

Henry was exhausted. It must have been the emotional stress, because he hadn't done anything strenuous. Under protest, he submitted to the physical examination. He was extremely embarrassed, but the doctors were professional and tried to make him as comfortable as possible. They asked whether he wanted his mom to be there or leave the room.

One nurse stood by him and engaged him in casual conversation to distract him from the examination. The doctor performing the examination kept Henry informed on what he was doing in a calm, informative monotone that helped ease the embarrassment.

Then he talked for what seemed like hours to counselors from the Crisis Center. His mouth was so dry, he felt like he could drink a gallon of water. When the doctor came to talk to his mom, he asked her to join him in the hallway. But they were just on the other side of the curtain, close enough that Henry could hear the conversation.

"Well, to start with, there's no trauma, like there would be if force was used. We can't tell at this time if there's been any nonviolent contact. We took forensic evidence, and that may give us a positive, but a negative doesn't mean there was no interference, just no physical evidence."

"And what about the shrinks? Can't they tell us anything?" Dorry demanded.

"A few thoughts, but nothing certain. He was pretty consistent about not remembering what happened to him as a child."

"But I know what happened to him back then," she pointed out.

"He may have blocked it out and truly not remember what happened. Kids are good at that."

"What about this time?" Dorry pressed.

"He didn't admit to anything happening."

"But he didn't before, either."

"Little kids don't know the difference between appropriate and inappropriate contact. Kisses, hugs, affectionate touching— how does a four or five-year-old know which are good and which are bad? And if he told you he was never touched, then he was told or threatened not to tell."

"And now?"

"Adolescence is a tough time too," the doctor waffled. "Hormones are on full-steam. An advance is made by a trusted adult and the kid can't shut off his own physical reaction, so he thinks it was consensual. He's confused and embarrassed. He doesn't want anyone to know that he had those kinds of feelings, so he won't tell."

"You think that about Henry?"

"He's confused. We know that much. Someone he loves has been accused of hurting him. He may not know whether anything inappropriate occurred. He hasn't been hurt physically. Maybe he hasn't been interfered with either; they can't tell for sure. He should have ongoing counseling to help him sort things out."

"You don't know any more now than I did when I brought him in," Dorry's voice rose plaintively.

"Sorry. It's not black and white. Your best bet is to spend some time with him, talking."

She snorted. "Henry and I don't talk."

"Teens can be hard to talk to," the doctor agreed sympathetically.

12

———————

When Henry thought back to his early memories of Frank, he had no recollection of anything bad. The idea that Frank could have done anything to him, that he could be a pedophile, was ridiculous. It made no sense.

Henry remembered trips to the zoo, walking to the park, doing things at home like making popsicles, doing crafts, or watching TV before bed. Henry didn't remember much about his mother during that time. She had been younger, less care-worn. He vaguely remembered that she used to cook meals, wake him up in the morning to get him off to school, and hang his school art projects on the fridge. She used to walk to the school to pick him up.

Henry pressed on, digging into the memories. Had Frank ever hurt him? Frank hadn't done anything. His mother was wrong. She had seen and heard what she wanted to, something that her brain had twisted into something dirty or sick. It wouldn't be the first time that she read too much into a situation. Henry was just little. Maybe Frank had been helping him in the bathtub or on the toilet. Maybe Henry had been sick and Frank had been helping him change his clothes. Dorry had just been confused, that was all.

She had taken an innocent, loving relationship and made it out to be something sick and depraved. What kind of person did that? When Henry had met Frank again, he hadn't felt bad or ashamed. He felt like he had come home. He felt love and acceptance.

Now she had taken that away and put something ugly in its place. She was so jealous of Frank's place as a father figure that she had taken him away from Henry.

———

Henry went back to school with relief, glad to get away from the house and his mother's reproachful gaze. He wanted to get back to the routine and not think about Frank. He wouldn't have to think of anything serious or upsetting.

He was sitting in the cafeteria staring at his books as if he was studying, although he wasn't really looking at them. He was watching for one of the guys that he sometimes hung around with, just wanting some undemanding company, but no one was around.

"Hey, Henry," someone shouted.

Henry looked up. It was Trent, and Henry wasn't excited about getting attention from him. Trent was one of those who got popular by stepping all over the unpopular. His long blond hair had probably taken hours to blow dry and arrange. He always wore the latest fashions. Henry looked down at his books, ignoring Trent.

"Henry," Trent's voice was suggestive, "I hear you're looking for a new *boyfriend*."

Henry's heart sank. Trent's voice carried over the general buzz of the cafeteria, and everybody quieted to listen. Everybody was turning around to look at him.

"'Cause I hear your last one got thrown in the clink," Trent went on.

Henry had no idea how he had found out about Frank.

Who had seen what happened? Who had known what Frank was on parole for? It wasn't in the papers, but somebody in the neighborhood obviously knew what had happened and spread it around.

"He's not my boyfriend," Henry said, but his voice was too quiet, too weak. "He's not my boyfriend; he's my dad."

Trent looked momentarily taken aback, but his surprise didn't last long. "You got a pervert for a dad?" he demanded loudly.

Henry sank deeper into his seat. He stared at his books, wishing he could sink right down into the print.

"He didn't do anything," Henry protested. "He didn't do any of that stuff that they said."

But it just added fuel to Trent's fire. People like Trent didn't back off because their target was squirming. The more you protested, the more they enjoyed it, and the harder they pushed.

13

Henry opened the door to the hamster cage and trickled food into the bowl. There was no movement from the nest in the corner.

"Chipper, come'ere," he called softly, clicking his tongue. "Come on."

Still no familiar twitch and sniffing nose. Henry put his hand in to rouse Chipper. He touched a cold, stiff body. He recoiled, jerking his hand back out and scratching it on the cage.

Henry sat down on the edge of his bed, overwhelmed. Everything was falling apart. He'd lost Frank again. Everybody at school figured he'd had some improper relationship with an older man. His mom was hardly able to look at him. His pet dead. Bobby was about the only one who hadn't started treating him differently, and he was teething to beat the band, so he was grumpy eighty percent of the time he was awake. It was all just too much for one person to handle at a time. It was just too much.

The days passed excruciatingly slowly. Henry hated going to school and hated being at home. There was no reprieve anywhere.

At the end of the week, Clint was home when Henry got in. Henry looked around, frowning.

"Ma home?" he questioned.

"No, she's gone out."

"And Bobby?"

"Yeah. She took him to that play center at the mall."

"Oh," Henry tried to figure out what to do. Go in his room and do his homework? Clint didn't usually stay around when the house was empty. Henry wasn't used to being alone with him. He was awkward, not sure how to behave.

"Your ma wanted me to have a talk with you," Clint said.

Henry frowned at him, not understanding. His brows drew down and he shook his head uncertainly. "A talk," Henry repeated. What was this? What was happening now?

Clint rolled his eyes. "*The Talk*," he said significantly. "You know, the birds 'n' the bees."

Henry grimaced and shifted uncomfortably from one foot to the other. "I always figured you the type to do that by taking your kid to a hooker on his sixteenth birthday," he offered.

For a moment, Clint looked stunned. Then he burst into laughter, the tension broken. "You're some kid!" he guffawed. He dabbed at the corners of his eyes and continued to snicker. "But you're not sixteen yet, huh?"

Henry shook his head. "Yeah, too bad. But I already know all that stuff. We learn it in school, you know," he hoped that Clint would just agree and let it go. Clint didn't need to explain anything.

Clint nodded. "I know you've been taught all the biological stuff, but there's more to it than that. There's a lot to understand. It can be… confusing."

Henry sighed. "Ma's still fussing about Frank. But nothing happened. I swear."

"Doesn't matter," Clint said flatly, "you still gotta know." He was silent for a moment, casting about for what to say, for how to introduce the topic. "A turn-on's a turn-on, whether it comes from the cute girl next door or a dirty old man. Just because you... have feelings... it doesn't mean that you're... something you're not..."

Henry's face heated, flooded with embarrassment. He clapped a hand to his forehead and swore under his breath. He didn't usually cuss, but he didn't know what to say. Clint was going to tell him, whether he wanted to hear or not. No matter how uncomfortable it was for both of them.

Henry tried to look attentive and just nod his head while focusing his mind on something else.

14

The doorbell rang. Henry frowned. In the neighborhood, people generally knocked and walked in. He wiped his hands on the towel thrown over his shoulder and picked Bobby up from the highchair. Henry went to the door and opened it. A couple of cops. Henry looked them over as they quickly sized him up. Henry saw by their eyes that, like the store clerks at the mall, they discounted him as no threat. Just a spindly, geeky boy.

"Are you Henry Thomas?" one of them questioned.

Henry nodded. "Yeah. What's going on?"

"Are your folks home?"

"No. Just me."

They exchanged glances, communicating with each other in silence. The taller one continued. "There was a complaint issued about you by Trent Lang, a boy at your school."

"A complaint?" Henry repeated. "What does that mean?"

"Can we come in?"

"I guess." Henry stepped back from the door, motioning them in. He was going to take them into the living room, but he hesitated at the kitchen doorway.

"I have dinner cooking," he explained.

"We'll come in there."

Henry nodded. He put Bobby back in the highchair and checked the pots on the stove while the cops looked around, out of place.

"So, what happened?" Henry prompted. "With Trent."

"He found a nasty surprise in his locker."

"Yeah? What?" Henry asked, stirring a pot.

"You didn't hear?" the other cop challenged.

"No… I'm sort of out of touch with the grapevine. Too much of a geek." Henry shrugged.

"I see. Well, maybe you could guess," the tall one suggested.

"What was in his locker?" It sounded sort of like Bilbo's riddle to Gollum in *The Hobbit*. *What's in my pocket?* How was Henry supposed to know? "I dunno. Drugs? A week-old lunch? Porn?"

"A dead hamster, dripping with what turned out to be ketchup and a threatening note."

"Really?" Henry covered his mouth, but not before a snicker escaped. "What'd he do? Gross out?"

"He was sick. And very upset. Is that the reaction you were hoping for?"

Henry suppressed his humor, sobering up and adopting a serious expression. "He really thinks I did it? Why me?"

"Apparently, there was quite a scene in the cafeteria a few days ago. He said things that upset you."

Quite a scene was one way to describe it. Henry had no doubt that all of the teachers and administrators had heard about the things that Trent had said. Certainly, all of the students had. Things weren't easy for Henry at school. Even the boys he had counted as his friends before avoided him. They didn't want to be seen talking with him. He was completely isolated, a pariah, thanks to Trent.

"I'm not the first," he commented. "Ask around. He's a jerk and a bully. He's upset a lot of people."

He saw by their eyes that they already knew that.

"Yeah, he made me mad," Henry admitted. "He would have ruined my reputation, if I'd had one to start with. But I don't really care what anyone else thinks. I know the truth. I don't go to school for the social life."

"Well, that's a healthy attitude. You do well at school?"

"I get good marks. I do my homework."

"Do you have a hamster?" the shorter one questioned.

"Sure."

"Can we see it?"

Henry took Bobby out of the highchair. "I guess. It's in my room."

He led the way. In his bedroom, he put Bobby down on the floor and opened the door of Chipper Two's cage.

"Chipper, come'ere Chipper," he called quietly, and picked the hamster up. He held the soft ball of fur against his chest. "You think I'd kill a helpless creature to make a point? To get back at Trent for embarrassing me?"

"That was the suggestion," the tall one admitted.

"That's like how a serial killer or something starts out, isn't it? Vivisecting animals?"

"That's what they say."

"I would never do that." Henry put the hamster back in the cage.

"You don't have a record, do you, Henry?"

"Are you kidding? I've never even had a detention at school."

"And no one's ever accused you of this kind of thing before?"

"No," Henry shook his head. "Trent teases a lot of people. Maybe I'm at the top of the suspect list, but I ll bet he's ticked off a lot of other people."

"Who do you think would do something like that?" the cop asked, as if they were friends, as if he really thought Henry might have some insight into it.

"I don't know anyone that well. It's my first year in high

school, I don't know a lot of the kids. But then, they say you can't tell, even if it is someone you know real well."

"That's been my experience. People who do these kinds of things usually keep their deviance hidden pretty deep."

"So, what are you going to do? You're not gonna charge me or tell my mom, are you?"

"I don't think we have any evidence to charge you. Just one person's suspicion."

Henry nodded, relieved.

"But I do think your mom should know what's going on. She should know you're having trouble at school with this guy."

Henry was uncomfortable. "My mom…"

"I'm sure you won't be in trouble. But it helps parents to know what's going on in their kid's life."

"But my mom's sort of… she can't handle stress. She's not emotionally well."

"What do you mean?"

"If things don't go good, she gets sick. We have to protect her from things that might upset her."

"But she's well enough to take care of you," the officer said tentatively, looking around to re-evaluate whether he needed to call Social Services in.

"As long as everything's cool," Henry assured him. "I'm old enough to look after myself. When I was little, sometimes I had to go into foster care until she could get back on track. I don't want that to happen again."

The cop shrugged. "Well, you're most experienced in dealing with her. You can decide what to tell her."

Henry breathed out. "Thanks."

"If you continue to have problems with this Trent character, you let someone know what's going on, okay?" the cop suggested. "Sometimes things can get out of hand. I wouldn't want it to escalate to violence."

"Okay."

"Okay. Nice to meet you, Henry."

Henry escorted them out to the door. He saw them shake their heads as they walked away and heard a murmur of conversation between them: "…nice kid… responsible."

Henry hummed to himself as he finished making dinner. He couldn't stop himself from grinning.

15

Henry waited nervously, the clanging of the heavily barred doors behind him making his heart race. His stomach was tied in knots. Eventually, a guard rejoined him and took him into the visiting area, where Frank sat on the other side of a pane of bulletproof glass, with an old-style phone on either side. When Frank saw him, his face twisted into a scowl. He picked up his phone receiver.

"Henry. What are you doing here?" he demanded roughly.

"I wanted to see you. Hear your side of the story," Henry explained, hurt by Frank's manner. Frank had known he was coming. He'd added Henry to his visitor list.

"My side of the story?" Frank repeated. "I wasn't supposed to be around kids. I knew that," he said bluntly. "I broke parole."

"No, I get that. I mean... before. Did Ma just make that up?" he urged.

"You don't remember," Frank said, with a jerky shake of his head.

"I remember lots of things," Henry said softly. "You being like a dad to me. I don't remember anything... *wrong.*"

Frank looked different in prison. He had ragged gray

whiskers like he hadn't shaved in a week. He looked like he had lost weight. Instead of being fatherly, he looked like a convict. Was it because of his attitude, how he felt locked up in prison instead of free? Or was it that Henry was looking at him with fresh eyes, clouded by suspicion?

"I didn't think you remembered," Frank said. He swallowed hard, his Adam's apple bobbing down and up again. "You said you remembered and I thought that… Never mind what I thought," he said abruptly. "I think a lot of things. I thought… things were okay between us."

"You never did anything," Henry asserted.

"I did love you like a son, Henry. I helped to raise you. And that just makes it that much worse." Frank's voice was rough, harsh. Despondent.

Henry waited, wanting to know but not wanting to ask. He couldn't put it into words. He couldn't accuse Frank. Couldn't rip his heart out.

"How do you think I feel?" Frank demanded. "Knowing that inside, I'm… a monster. I would do something and then be so sick and ashamed, so disgusted with myself. I would swear that it would never happen again. And I meant it. But the temptation was just too much for me. The monster would poke its head out again. I was almost relieved when your mom found out. I thought I could start over somewhere else, and it would be different."

"But it wasn't."

"No. I still had the same feelings. And I let myself be caught again. I wanted them to lock me up."

"Why?" Henry questioned.

"I didn't want to hurt kids. But I couldn't stop myself."

"Why did they let you out again?"

"I got lots of counseling in here, lots of help. I thought I was over it. That I didn't have to worry about… the monster in me coming out again. But when I saw you and held Bobby—it all came back. The temptations were getting too strong. When I would touch you on the shoulder… look at you across the table… I didn't know how to approach you. You said you remembered, and I didn't know what kind of relationship you wanted or expected."

Henry swallowed. The awkwardness that would pop up between him and Frank in odd moments… the look that Frank would give him… uncertain and questioning…

"What did you do to me?" Henry asked hoarsely.

"If you don't remember," Frank questioned. "Why do you want to know the details?"

"I always thought you were my friend. Now… I want to know the truth."

"You don't want to hear. And I don't want to put it into words," Frank said, shaking his head. His eyes were shiny with tears.

"I'll find out," Henry countered. There were ways he could find out. It didn't have to be from Frank himself.

"Not from me," Frank said steadily, staring at him. "You won't hear any details from me."

16

Henry sat in the cafeteria eating his sandwich, not looking at or talking to anyone else. He had his elbows on the table, holding onto the sandwich with both hands, and he just stared at it.

"Henry. Hey, Henry."

He became aware that someone was trying to get his attention, and looked up. It was Tony. His face was open and friendly.

"Yeah?" he answered cautiously.

"Can you do me a favor?"

"I dunno," Henry stalled. "What?"

"Well, my brother, he invited me to this party at his frat house. If I go by myself, I'm just gonna be some guy's kid brother. But if I go with some friends, maybe I can have a good time." The last words sounded like a question. Tony raised his eyebrows hopefully.

Henry was surprised by the invitation. "I dunno. I can't really go out at night," Henry said, thinking of Bobby.

Tony raised his brows. "Never?"

"Maybe," Henry said, not wanting to make Tony more curious about his life. "I'll try. Let me know where and when."

"Sure," Tony agreed, breaking into a cheerful grin.

"Who else is going?" Henry asked.

"Andrew, for sure. One or two others, maybe. I don't know that many people yet."

Henry nodded. "I'll see what I can do. I'm not sure."

"Great! Hope you can make it!"

———

Dorry was watching TV. Henry hadn't seen Clint around. Maybe he was working or out at the bar. Henry stood in the doorway, watching her for a few minutes, trying to get up his courage.

"Mom?" he said tentatively.

She looked up from the TV show. "What is it, honey?"

"Can I talk to you about something?"

She muted the TV. "Yeah. What's up?"

"It's about Frank."

Her face fell, smile disappearing like it had never been there to start with. "I don't want to hear anything else about Frank," she growled.

"I lied to you," Henry confessed.

"I know you did."

"He… confused me. But… it's true… what you said," Henry spoke with difficulty, stumbling over his words and trying to sort out what to say to her.

"You might have to testify in court. If they lay additional charges." She looked into his face. "Is that what you want?"

"I don't know if I could," Henry said quietly.

She nodded understandingly. "I could hardly stand to testify all those years ago." She picked up her drink and swallowed a few gulps, staring at the muted TV show instead of looking at Henry. "It was one of the hardest things I've ever done. But I had to do it to make sure they put him away. It was the only way."

"But he's already behind bars. I don't have to testify, do I?"

"No. You don't." She looked at him wistfully and he didn't think she was going to say anything further. "My poor sweetie," she murmured. "When you were a baby, I figured we could put this behind us. You'd grow up, start to forget, not be permanently scarred by it. But now, this time… you're going to carry it with you forever, into every relationship."

Henry was embarrassed. He fussed with his collar, straightening it and scraping at a fleck of food on his shirt with his nail.

"I'm not scarred," he objected, his face hot and sweat making his shirt cling to him. "It wasn't that big a deal. Just… touching… experimenting. Not… not anything… serious."

"Do you know what he did when you were little?" she asked in a strangled tone.

Henry shook his head. He bit his tongue before letting slip that Frank wouldn't tell him. She didn't know that he had been to see Frank, getting into the prison with a forged letter of permission.

"Do you want to know?" she questioned, looking away from Henry, trying to keep her composure.

Henry nodded. "Yeah, sort of," he said uncomfortably.

He didn't know why he couldn't remember. It seemed like a betrayal that his brain would hide the details away, making him think that his time with Frank had been innocent and special. Instead of… whatever it was. He couldn't help thinking that everyone was just overreacting, misinterpreting something that had a perfectly innocent explanation.

"I can't talk to you about it," Dorry said, licking dry lips and swallowing. "It's too hard. But I have copies of court documents. If you want to read them."

Henry breathed out. He could stand that. He didn't have to listen to her maligning Frank; he could just read it from clinical, unemotional pages.

"Yeah. Just show me where they are and if I want to read them, I can."

"Okay," she agreed.

17

Henry checked again to see that he had everything that Bobby would need in the diaper bag, and some extra just in case. Did he want to go through with it? He'd never been invited to a party, much less a frat party. If he didn't take the opportunity, it might never come again. It was his one chance to do something like the popular kids, to be one of the in crowd.

Henry walked up to the decrepit building and knocked on the door. An older, heavy woman answered the door. She looked Henry over and motioned him in.

"You'd better come inside."

Henry stepped in. There was a lot of noise inside, women and children's voices, and baby's cries. The air smelled like warm soup and sweat.

"I need to leave Bobby here for a while," Henry said uncertainly.

"How long? This is only short-term respite."

"I know. Just a few hours overnight. I'll pick him up later tonight or in the morning."

"While you go on a date?" she questioned suspiciously, studying him.

"I was told 'no questions asked' if I brought him here."

She flushed a little and nodded, grimacing. "You're absolutely right," she agreed. "We don't get a lot of young men here —usually only women. You need someone to look after him for a while. Bringing him here is a responsible choice."

Henry breathed a sigh of relief. He wiped his forehead.

"What's baby's name?" she questioned briskly, pulling out a paper form and a pen.

"Bobby."

"And is he your son?"

Henry hesitated. "Does it make a difference?" he queried.

"No."

"He's my brother."

"Mom's not around?"

Henry shrugged and didn't give her any details.

"Okay," she said, not pushing for more information. "You have everything we'll need in the bag?"

"Yeah."

"Food, bottles, diapers?"

"Some extra clothes, too," Henry said, nodding.

"Great. Let's get the two of you tagged."

"Tagged?" Henry repeated.

"For security, hon'. We will only release a child to the person who brought him in or to the police. Someone who shows up demanding access, too bad. We give you each a bracelet. They have to match for the child to be released."

She got out a couple of plastic, colored bracelets and wrote an identification number on each.

"Couldn't someone just copy the bracelets? What if I have to take it off and you see it's been cut?"

"You give me a password. Something you won't forget, but that no one else will know. Not a birthdate."

"Frank."

"Not a pet's name or something someone would guess?"

"No," Henry shook his head. No one would ever guess that

he'd use Frank's name. He wasn't sure why he was, but he told himself it was so nobody could guess.

"Does Bobby have any medical conditions?"

"No."

"Anyone you need to keep away from? That we should call the police about if they show up?"

He was lucky that he didn't have to deal with some stalker or ex-husband like some of the women who came here must. He might have the extra responsibility of taking care of Bobby, but at least he didn't have to worry about some abusive partner chasing after him. He had it easy compared to that.

"No."

"Okay."

Bobby was fast asleep, long lashes resting on his rosy cheeks, lips pursed. Henry kissed him on the forehead and left.

———

Tony was hyped up, excited about going to the party. He had a crazy grin and was bouncing around on his heels, making jokes and then laughing at them. Henry wasn't so sure how he felt. Mostly nervous. Out of place. But a little excited too.

"I hope some of the others meet us there," Tony said. "I want to have a good time. I mean, you and me will have a good time, but even better if there's more of us," he added quickly.

Henry nodded.

"Yeah, that'd be good," he agreed. He looked at his watch. "Let's go," he encouraged, anxious to be on their way before he could change his mind. Tony looked at the time on his phone and nodded.

"Bus should be here in five minutes," he said.

They left the house—Tony bouncing, and Henry walking sedately—and waited at the bus stop.

———

Ned looked like a mirror image of Tony, only older. Henry knew instantly that he was Tony's brother.

"Hey li'l' brother," Ned greeted Tony, when he saw the two of them come in. "Glad you made it. You and your friend go help yourself to some Jell-O."

"Jell-O?" Henry repeated, his brows drawing down in a frown.

Ned laughed at his look.

"Jell-O shooters. It's a frat thing. They're made with alcohol instead of water."

"Oh. Yeah."

Henry felt stupid. He had heard of Jell-O shooters before. But he'd never had them. Ned laughed again and pointed.

"Over there. Just remember it ain't like your mom's Jell-O," he warned.

Tony and Henry went over to the Jell-O tub and tried some out. Tony grimaced.

"They're not so bad," he said, his wrinkled nose telling another story.

Henry shrugged. "I dunno. Kind of strange," he admitted.

There wasn't much for them to do yet, and they had a few more shooters before Andrew got there. He was with a girl.

"That's his sister," Tony said as he watched them approach with a scowl. "She's weird. I dunno what he brought her for."

Henry went to get them shooters. When he got back, Andrew's sister had cut her finger on something.

"Kiss it," she told Andrew, shoving her finger in his face.

Andrew turned his face away in distaste. "Get out of here, Liz!"

She pouted. "I said kiss it," she insisted in a baby voice, pushing the injury to his lips. "Do it," she insisted, clinging to his arm with her other hand.

Andrew kissed it impatiently and pushed her away. Henry was uncomfortable with the bizarrely intimate scene. He waited until the couple separated and then approached Andrew with the shooters. Since he'd gotten two, they each had one. Andrew caught Henry staring at him.

"What? I get a big zit on my nose?" he demanded in irritation.

"No. It's just… you and your sister…" Henry stumbled for the right words.

"What about us?" Andrew said impatiently, slurping down the Jell-O.

"You look like… you look like…"

Andrew shook his head. "How many of those have you had? Just what are you trying to say?"

The alcohol was too much for Henry. He tried to formulate a tactful question in his mind, but the words escaped his loose lips before he had a chance.

"You sleeping with her, or what?"

Andrew's eyes widened in shock, and his jaw dropped.

"How did you know that?" he questioned in astonishment.

Henry couldn't believe it.

"She's your sister!" he protested, drawing back from Andrew a step in horror.

"You think I don't know that?" Andrew whispered harshly, leaning close to him and breathing in his face. "You got no idea how much I want her to leave me alone!"

"Then just stay away from her," Henry insisted.

"You don't know how it is. It started when we were little. You know, playin' doctor, being curious. But as soon as we were old enough to know it was wrong, she started blackmailing me. Saying she'd tell what I'd done if I wouldn't do what she wanted."

"And she wanted you to…?"

"Yeah. I've tried to set her up with other guys to get her off my case. But no one wants anything to do with her," Andrew's voice cracked with emotion. He blinked rapidly then stared across the room at her.

Henry studied her.

"If she was better looking, I could get rid of her," Andrew said.

She wasn't ugly. But she wasn't pretty, either. She was flat-chested, had a long, angular nose, and limp, straight hair. She wasn't wearing any makeup.

"I would do anything to get rid of her. I wish someone would teach her a lesson. Show her what it's like, what she does."

Henry shook his head uncomfortably.

"I can't believe it."

"It's not my fault," Andrew maintained.

"If it's her, why don't you just tell someone?"

"You think anyone's gonna believe she's the aggressor? I'm older and I'm the guy. No one's ever gonna believe me. Not ever."

18

Henry awoke all at once to a cacophony of sound and light. The light hurt his eyes, sliced into his head. His eyes teared, and the noise was horrendous. He tried to cover his face to block it all out, disoriented, but someone grabbed him firmly by the arm, barking in his ear.

"Get up, kid. Come on. On your feet."

Getting to his feet was a worse mistake than waking up. Nausea washed over him, and his stomach lurched. He forced his eyes open. The man holding his arm was a uniformed cop. Other cops were escorting leftover partiers to the door. There was shouting and banging and all kinds of confusion.

Henry stopped at the door, and the cop impatiently pushed him over the doorstep. Henry looked down the steps and nausea overtook him. He doubled over, stomach heaving.

"Come on," the cop growled, pushing him.

Henry grabbed the handrail, retching over the bushes. Others pushed past him. Everybody walked like zombies, still half asleep, drunk or hungover.

Eventually, Henry's stomach settled down, and once again, the cop took his arm firmly and escorted him into a squad car.

———

At the police station, Henry sat alone in a small, gray interrogation room and tried to sort things out. It was some kind of bust, obviously. Drugs? He was clean other than alcohol, which should be out of his system by now. Maybe the frat house was doing illegal froshing, although Henry hadn't seen anything the previous night.

Henry's head was still whirling. He just wanted to put down his head and go to sleep. He'd obviously had too many of those little Jell-O shooters the night before. He hadn't realized that they were so potent.

The door opened and an officer came in. He was short and slim, his face mapped with fine lines of experience.

"Hi, kid," he greeted casually. "Jim Barnes. How's it going?"

"Umm, okay, I guess."

"Good. You're looking a little green there. The officer who brought you in said you were sick."

"Yeah. Too much to drink, I guess," Henry admitted.

"That'll do it. You want a coffee or anything?"

Henry wrinkled his nose. He'd never developed a taste for coffee. "No."

"Juice? Water?"

"Maybe... like, some soda would settle my stomach," Henry suggested.

"I'll see what I can do." Barnes left the room for a moment and then returned. "Someone will bring it in a minute," he advised.

"Thanks."

"So. Your name?"

"Henry Thomas."

Barnes wrote it down in a small notepad. "How old are you, Henry? A little young to be at a frat party, aren't you?"

"A guy I know, his brother invited him, and I went along." Henry glanced around. "What's going on? Why're we here?"

"What can you tell me about what happened at the party last night?" Barnes questioned, not answering Henry's questions.

"I don't know," Henry's shoulders lifted in a shrug. "Music, dancing, talking. Nothing much."

"Drinking?"

"Not exactly. Jell-O shooters."

"Drugs?" Barnes suggested.

"I didn't see any. No one offered me anything."

"Sex?"

Henry felt his face heat up. He shifted uncomfortably. "I suppose. Plenty of kids making out."

"You?"

"No."

"Are you sure?"

Henry considered. He didn't remember a lot of what had happened last night. There were a lot of blanks. A few fleeting images, though, made him unsure whether he could answer honestly.

"I don't remember a lot of last night. I think maybe I got together with a girl."

"A college girl?" Barnes questioned skeptically.

Henry tried to put a face on the images. It was all so foggy. He remembered—what? Going upstairs with someone… but it was all so vague and unclear.

"I'm not sure. I think it was my friend's sister… maybe."

Barnes was watching him like a hawk to determine if he was telling the truth. Henry still didn't know what all of the questions were about.

"How old would she be?" Barnes questioned.

"I dunno, she's younger… maybe thirteen."

"And what exactly did you do with her?"

Henry tried to summon up details, sweating. He swallowed strenuously and wondered what had happened to the soda.

"I don't know what this is about," he protested. "Why does

it matter if I made out with Liz? Lots of people were fooling around."

Barnes studied him for several long moments. Then he threw a glossy photo down on the table in front of Henry.

It was Liz. Gray, eyes shut, obviously dead. Henry's stomach twisted and he was really scared for the first time. Liz was dead. He'd been with her. Maybe he'd been the last one with her. They knew that. Henry's head whirled and he covered his face with both hands, dangerously dizzy and nauseated.

19

Henry wasn't sure if he blacked out or if no time had passed. Barnes was at his side, taking his pulse with strong, dry fingers, talking to him in a quiet, urgent tone.

"You're okay. Just take it easy. Head between your knees."

Barnes pulled Henry's chair out from the table and firmly pushed Henry's head down. Henry complied.

"You okay?" Barnes questioned. "You have any medical conditions we should know about?"

"No… no, it's just the hangover… the shock…" His voice broke and a tear escaped his eye. "I can't remember what happened!"

"Just sit and take it easy for a minute," Barnes soothed.

Henry took deep breaths, trying to settle down. Trying to remember those few moments with Lizzy.

"Let's take it from the top," Barnes suggested when Henry was breathing easier and sat up, trying to steady himself again. "You remember being at the party, drinking Jell-O shooters. Do you remember when Liz got there?"

"Yeah. With Andrew, her brother."

"Did you see her after that? Did she stick with your group?" Barnes suggested.

"No. Andrew didn't want her there. Told her to get lost."

He realized that didn't make Andrew sound good and shrugged uncomfortably.

"Then when did you make out?" Barnes reminded him.

Henry searched his memory but could not remember what had happened.

"I'll go see what happened to that soda," Barnes said abruptly and walked out.

Henry sat uncertainly. He moved his chair closer to the table again, resting his elbows. It was a long time before Barnes returned. He didn't have the promised soda. Henry was getting very dry. He could really use a drink to help him to settle down.

"So," Barnes said, with no mention of the missing beverage. "You remember anything else?"

"No." Henry shook his head.

"You took Liz upstairs."

"Um, I guess."

"Why?"

Henry felt himself flushing. He shrugged self-consciously. "To make out, I guess." Then suddenly, it came back to him in a flash. "No—it wasn't. It was to clean her up. She had too many shooters, threw up this green Jell-O all over herself. Made a disgusting mess. She was bawling like a baby. Everyone was just laughing at her. Wouldn't get near her. I took her upstairs to help her wash up."

Barnes nodded. Henry could see this was no surprise to him. Someone else must have already told him that part.

"So you took her up to the main bathroom?"

"No, it was too busy. Ned said I could use the one off the master bedroom."

"Half bath? Shower?" Barnes questioned.

"No, it was huge. Full bath. Like, this great big jacuzzi thing."

Barnes sat back and looked at him.

"Tell me what happened."

Henry frowned.

"I don't remember everything… had to get her clothes off, they were covered with green slime… thought I'd wash them in the sink and throw them in the frat's dryer. Maybe one of the fraternity members could lend her something until they were dry."

"And where was she while you were washing her stuff in the sink?"

"In the tub, I guess," Henry closed his eyes and tried to picture it, tried to remember. He could remember her singing in the tub, in a high, wobbly voice, as she splashed around. "Yeah, she was in the tub, washing off. I was afraid she was too drunk to be in the water. She could have an accident, drowned or something."

"So you got in with her?" Barnes said.

Henry shook his head. "No, I took off my socks and shirt, rolled up my pant legs. I just stepped in at the edge and tried to get her to come out."

"And?"

Henry licked his lips, parched. He didn't want to talk about it. He was inexperienced with girls and the encounter with Liz had been unexpected. Henry could only remember bits and pieces. He had yet to assimilate what had happened.

"Liz didn't want to come out. She kept trying to pull me in." Henry couldn't go on. Sweat gathered at his temples and trailed down his face. Barnes was silent for a long time, just waiting. Waiting for him to fill in the silence and say what had happened. "She was kissing, touching, teasing. I took off my pants and got in with her," Henry admitted. "Made out."

Barnes nodded slowly.

"And the two of you had relations. Then what?"

Henry could remember the warmth of the jacuzzi. The feeling of fuzzy well-being. Her silly singing and teasing. Feeling really good. He couldn't remember what had happened next.

"I don't know." It was a blank.

"How did she die, Henry?"

"I don't think I could have been there. I don't remember anything."

"What do you remember?"

"I don't know. I can't remember draining the tub... getting dressed again... going to sleep... any of it."

"You were there," Barnes told him.

"I don't think I was," Henry protested. If he had been there, why didn't he remember?

"You hit her over the head," Barnes snapped. "Why? Did she fight you? Change her mind? Or that's just what pushes your buttons?"

Henry was shocked. He licked his lips again. They were like sandpaper.

"No, no, I never hit her. I'd never do that," he protested.

"How much do you drink normally?"

"Not that much," Henry said hesitantly.

"This is the first time you've been out drinking like this?"

"Yeah."

"Then how do you know how you would treat her with some firewater in you?"

"I'm just not like that," Henry said lamely.

"How can you know what you're like?" Barnes' voice was harsh, accusing. "People do things when they've been drinking that they would never think of doing sober. Are you the kind of guy who would normally climb into bed with a girl you'd never met before? One who'd just been throwing up all over herself?"

Henry swallowed, a lump in his throat. "No," it came out a whisper, and he tried again. "No, but... I'm not great with girls... they're not usually interested in me."

"Which brings us to a whole other facet of this thing. Who slipped her Rohypnol? You or one of your buddies?"

"Rohypnol?" Henry said.

"Date rape drug of choice."

"I didn't give her anything. You gotta believe me. I was just trying to take care of her, help her out."

"You killed her."

"No. I just fooled around with her," Henry said firmly, feigning confidence that he did not have. "I never hit her."

"You had a fight, or maybe you were angry because of the amount you drank. It's better if you tell us now. Get it off your chest. I can't help you if you lie to me," Barnes urged.

Henry rubbed his eyes, fighting tears. "I'm telling the truth," he whined.

"How much did you have to drink?" Barnes questioned, taking another tack.

"I don't know. It didn't seem like a lot."

"How many shooters?"

"Half a dozen, maybe."

"Do you usually have blackouts when you drink?"

"I… I don't know… "

"This is the first time you've had alcohol," Barnes divined.

"Yeah," Henry admitted.

"First time you've been with a girl, too?"

"Uh-huh."

"I see. It's a confusing time for you. Unexpected emotions. You don't know what it might bring out. You didn't know this was going to happen. It's okay. Just tell me. We can work it out."

Henry rested his face in his hands, elbows on the table.

"Why don't you think it over a while," Barnes suggested. He got up and walked out.

Henry sat there, unmoving. The tears he had held back with Barnes there started to flow. He didn't try to stop them. He just couldn't control it. Henry felt like he was falling apart. He knew he couldn't have killed Liz. He couldn't hurt anybody. Yes, he'd been drinking, but he knew he couldn't have killed her.

Barnes was so sure. What evidence did he have? What were the others telling him?

Henry tried to dry his tears and sort it out. He had to approach it objectively. He had to protect himself, defend himself. Henry couldn't let Barnes force him into a corner he couldn't get out of.

20

────────

When Barnes finally got back, Henry had control of himself. He wiped his eyes and nose on his shirt. He bit his lip to keep his emotions in check.

"I want you to tell me the rest," Barnes said. "Are you ready?"

"I think I need a lawyer," Henry said evenly.

Barnes raised his brows, but didn't look surprised. "That's your right," he acknowledged. "But you haven't been charged with anything."

"You think I did it," Henry pointed out.

"I know you did it," Barnes agreed flatly. "I'm just waiting for the rest of the forensic evidence and the autopsy results to come in."

"Autopsy? Doesn't that take a long time?"

"We should have the preliminary results today."

"I don't want to stay here. Do I have to stay?"

Barnes considered this. "I think it would be a good idea for you to stick around until all of this is cleared up," he said obliquely.

"But do I have to?" Henry pressed.

"No. You don't. I'll get all of your contact information and have your parents pick you up."

"I don't want you to call my mom. I'll go home by myself. I know how to get around on the bus."

"You're a juvenile. I need to call her," Barnes said reasonably.

Henry shook his head. "My mom can't take it. She's not real stable."

"She's going to find out before too long," the officer pointed out.

"You're not charging me. You can't tell me what to do."

"Oh, you'll be charged, all right. By the end of the day. Then you'll be back here, your mom will know, and you'll be behind bars."

"I want to go now," Henry insisted, standing up.

Barnes shrugged and nodded. "All right."

———

Henry glanced behind himself again, self-conscious. Barnes had put a tail on him. Very obvious. They didn't want him running off before they could get the evidence to arrest him. Henry stopped at the shelter and picked up Bobby, not explaining why he was so late getting there. They looked him over and didn't pursue it. He probably looked pretty rough.

He went home. There was nowhere else to go. No one was home. Henry put Bobby down to play and turned on the TV. He was too worried to study. He knew he should be doing his homework, but he knew he wouldn't be able to concentrate on it.

They thought he had killed Liz. They were intent on putting him in jail. What had happened? If he hadn't killed her, who had? Would they be able to figure out the truth?

If Henry went to jail, who would look after Bobby? His mom couldn't. Clint couldn't; he was working. Bobby would end up getting neglected during the day when his mom was supposed to be there and hurt at night if he woke up Clint. Henry would have to convince Social Services to take Bobby away, put him in a foster home until he was old enough to look after his own needs.

Henry was going to go to jail just like Frank. Suddenly, he wasn't so angry with Frank. He felt sorry for him. Maybe Frank didn't deserve to be in jail. Maybe it had just been a misunderstanding, like the baffling situation with Liz.

Henry went to his mom's room, where she had told him the court papers on Frank were. He sat on her bed for a few minutes, looking at the file box they were in before deciding to open it and find out what had really happened.

———

Henry packed Bobby's diaper bag and put him in the stroller and went out for a walk. He didn't start out with a plan; that came later. Initially, he just wanted to get out of the stifling stillness of the house and clear his head.

Henry hadn't been to Andrew's house since they were little kids. But as he was walking, he remembered where it was. Andrew could help. He could tell Henry what he didn't remember. Andrew would tell the cops that Henry would never kill anyone.

There were a lot of cars in front of the house. Henry rang the doorbell. A woman answered the door, looking solemn.

"Is Andrew here?" Henry questioned lowly, suddenly realizing that the house was in mourning. All of the cars, all of the people in the house talking in hushed tones.

"Just a moment."

She ducked back into the house, and Andrew came to the door a minute later. He looked terrible. His eyes were red-rimmed and swollen. It had been less than twenty-four hours since Henry had seen Andrew, but the boy looked like he hadn't eaten or slept in days.

Andrew stared at him through the screen door, then slammed it open and stepped out. "You got some nerve coming here!" he snarled.

"I just wanted to talk about what happened," Henry protested.

"What happened? You take Liz upstairs, and the next thing I know, she's dead! I thought you didn't come down because she was passed out, or you were making out, or something."

Henry opened his mouth and couldn't find the words to protest. "But—I didn't—"

"I told you I wished someone would teach her a lesson— but you went too far! You killed her! How could you kill Lizzy?" Andrew's voice rose to a scream. "You killed my baby sister!"

"I didn't—"

The door opened and a man stepped out. There were others behind him. They could obviously hear Andrew's shouting from the house.

"I think you'd better leave, son," the man told Henry.

"I didn't do it," Henry protested. "Andrew, you know I'm not that kind of guy!"

"You heard me, kid. Move on," the man repeated firmly.

Henry stood there, his feet rooted to the ground. He knew he should move, but he was frozen.

"Get out of here!" Andrew screamed.

Henry ran.

―――――

The doorbell rang. Henry laid on his bed and ignored it. He couldn't deal with any more visitors, especially if they were cops. He just needed to rest, to be by himself. They'd just have to come back.

"Henry," Barnes said from the bedroom doorway.

Henry jumped. He sat up and stared at Barnes. "What are you doing here? You can't break into my house!" he yelled.

"I didn't break in. The door was open. I guess you didn't hear me ring the bell."

"What do you want?" Henry questioned tiredly, leaning on his hand. "You came to arrest me now?"

"Well, the autopsy results came in."

Henry waited. If they were going to take him in, no protest was going to stop them now.

"I hear you went by your friend's house this afternoon," Barnes said, changing the subject.

"Yeah. And he thinks I did it," Henry spat bitterly.

"You were the last one to be with her. He knows that."

"I didn't hurt her," Henry insisted.

"The forensics guys found traces of blood in the bath," Barnes said.

Henry tried to remember. He knew he'd been in the tub with Liz. Had he gotten out and left her there? He couldn't remember anything after lounging in the tub with her, a tingly sense of well-being enveloping him.

"I just made out with her. There was no blood. Maybe it was someone else's blood, from some other time," Henry suggested.

"It was hers. We tested. She got the blow to her head when she fell and struck it on the faucet."

It took a minute to sink in.

"When she fell?" Henry repeated.

"Fell or was pushed. But the evidence does support a fall."

"Then you know I didn't kill her," Henry said.

"Somebody cleaned her and the bathroom up afterward. The blood was cleaned up. She was moved from the tub to the bed. Why was she moved?" Barnes challenged.

"I don't know. I don't remember. Maybe I—if it was me—maybe I didn't know she was hurt—or dead."

"She had a great gash in her head, bled like the dickens. How drunk were you?"

"I guess I must have been pretty bad," Henry admitted. "I can't remember."

"How many drinks did you have? How many shooters?"

"Half a dozen. I'm not really sure. I didn't think they had that much alcohol in them."

"There was the Rohypnol too."

"I didn't give it to her."

"No. One of the older boys admitted to spiking some of the drinks. What I mean is, you might have had Rohypnol too, and it can make you forget."

"So that's what happened? She just fell down and hurt herself, and I can't remember because of the drinks?"

"It could be."

Henry let his breath out in a long sigh. "I was starting to believe it."

Barnes studied him. "I'm sorry to have had to put you through all this. It's my job. If you're not guilty, I'm glad of it."

"You're still not sure?"

"It's early yet. There hasn't been a ruling of homicide or accidental death. If the ruling is accidental death, I'll be leaving you alone. But there's still more investigating to be done before that."

Henry nodded. "I'm glad you believe me."

"You seem like a decent kid, Henry. I don't like it when good kids get mixed up in things like this. I hope you'll stay away from situations like this in the future."

"I don't usually go out partying. I'm pretty much a loner."

"There's nothing wrong with having friends. Just be careful what you spend your time doing."

Henry nodded. "Yeah. I will."

21

Henry walked into the kitchen, still in the ragged sweats that he wore for pajamas. Dorry, sipping her coffee, looked him over slowly.

"You still not feeling well, sweetie?" she questioned.

Henry shook his head.

"No, not really," he said.

She felt his forehead. Henry pulled back from her touch.

"You've already missed three days of school," Dorry observed, "and I know how much you hate to miss school. I suppose I should take you to the doctor."

"No," Henry said. "It's getting better. I'll probably be okay for school tomorrow."

A movement in the kitchen doorway caught Henry's eye, and he turned with a jerk and saw Clint standing there. Clint leaned against the frame, his eyes glinting. His knowing look told Henry that he was savvy to what was going on. He knew that Henry wasn't really sick. He was just trying to avoid having to go back to school for as long as possible.

"I'll go back tomorrow," Henry repeated. "I'm starting to feel better."

"Okay," Dorry agreed. "Clint and I are going to go out. You can look after Bobby."

Henry nodded in agreement. Clint smirked at him and helped himself to coffee without comment.

———

Henry went to his classes the next day, avoiding meeting anyone's eyes or talking to anyone. He couldn't stand to see the accusation in their eyes, the knowledge of what had happened. He knew that the rumors of Liz's death and his possible involvement were already all over the school. Whispers followed him everywhere he went. His reputation—if he had one, still— would be gone. He was surprised that the school hadn't called him to say he could pursue his education elsewhere.

Some of his teachers wanted to talk to him about making up his assignments from the days he missed. Others just looked at him with fear in their eyes. Even the teachers thought he had done it.

But at lunch, he ran into Andrew. Henry and Andrew both just stood there, looking at each other. Henry didn't know what to say. He was half-expecting Andrew to haul off and punch him straight in the nose. After a long, awkward moment, Henry turned to go the other way.

"No, wait," Andrew stopped him with a hand on his arm.

Henry looked at Andrew, waiting.

"It's okay," Andrew said awkwardly. "The cops said it wasn't you. That officer, Barnes, he said it looked like it was just a freak accident."

Henry shrugged, staring down at his sneakers and the dirty tiles beneath his feet. "I'm really sorry," he said.

"I can't believe that she's really gone," Andrew said, his voice sounding strained. "I keep expecting her to come up behind me and start buggin' me like she always did. It's so quiet. I feel like

I'm the only one living in the house. I don't know if my folks just don't want to be around anymore, but… it echoes. I just bounce around like a pinball." He paused, "I don't know why I'm telling you this."

"Because I'm your friend," Henry said softly.

Andrew nodded. "Yeah. And you were there… other people, they don't want to talk about it. They say sorry and all, but they don't want to hear… about Liz. And about how it is."

"I wish it hadn't'a happened," Henry said. "I was just trying to help her out; I didn't know anything would happen."

"When you didn't come down right away, I thought you two hit the sheets, you know? I never thought anything was wrong until morning, when no one had seen you.'

Henry's face burned, right up to the tips of his ears. He shrugged hopelessly. "I was just trying to take care of her," he repeated.

———

After school, Henry walked into the quiet house, worn out. He checked in on Bobby and found him sleeping peacefully. Henry flopped down on his bed, too wiped out to even think about homework. The day had been emotionally exhausting. He drifted off to sleep quickly.

Henry awoke with a start when Clint got home. Henry got up blearily, rubbing his eyes.

"You making my dinner?" Clint demanded, looking around impatiently.

"Uh—I fell asleep."

"The kid stinks, too."

Henry looked at Bobby playing happily in his crib. Clint was right, of course. He obviously had a dirty diaper.

"Yeah. I'll change him and rustle something up to eat."

Clint nodded. "I'm hungry. Make it something quick."

"Okay."

Henry changed Bobby and left him to play in the crib. He looked through the fridge and cupboards, trying to figure out what to make. He should have gone grocery shopping. The kitchen was pretty bare. Henry pulled out some macaroni and cheese and a can of tomato sauce and went to work.

22

———

The girls paid more attention to Henry than they had before Liz died.

It was strange. The girls who used to occasionally talk shyly to him, the nice girls, now went out of their way to avoid him. That wasn't the strange part. It was all of the girls who hung around him now, talking and looking at him provocatively. Their eyes alight with curiosity and excitement. He had, as rumor had it, raped and murdered a girl, and instead of avoiding him, they seemed to feed off the danger of being around him. Their eyes sparkled at the risk. Groups of them quieted and eyed him speculatively when he walked past them in the hall. Whispers and giggles followed him as he left them behind.

One of them was Lana. She was a slim, sexy thing who previously would not have given Henry a second look. Henry found her irresistible. He felt powerful when she would give him those half-bold, half-downcast glances that qualified as flirting. At first, he was shy of her attention, not sure how to respond to the advances. That only seemed to encourage her more.

He didn't know much about Lana's history and background.

He didn't know what made her tick—or more importantly, what it was in her past that attracted her to a potentially dangerous offender.

She was hanging out with Henry at his locker after school. Henry looked at his watch.

"I gotta get home," he told her. "I got a baby to look after."

He expected her to be turned off by this. But her reaction was—what? Jealousy? Anger? Interest? He couldn't read her expression, but the information hadn't scared her off as he had expected.

"I'll come with you," she offered smoothly.

Henry hesitated, raising his eyebrows. Then he shrugged.

"If you want," he agreed. "My mom or Clint might be around, though."

"Just tell 'em you're tutoring me. You're smart, right?"

"I get by," Henry agreed, a chuckle rising up in his throat.

They headed for home. Henry had his hands in his pockets and she took his arm somewhat possessively after a couple of blocks, walking so closely stuck to his side that he had to slow down to avoid tripping over her.

There was no one at home. Henry went into his room and got Bobby out of the crib. Lana hung back while he changed Bobby's diaper and put him down to toddle around.

"Is he your..." Lana trailed off.

"My brother," Henry finished for her. "Half brother."

"Oh. How come nobody's looking after him?"

"I look after him."

"Huh." She looked around the house, "So what else do you do?"

Henry shrugged. "I got plenty to do."

Cooking, cleaning, studying. Nothing that she would be interested in.

"Since your folks aren't around," Lana said slyly. "You and me could spend some quality time together."

Henry swallowed. Did she mean what he thought she

meant? He'd never had a girl come onto him like that. Girls talked to him. Smiled at him occasionally. But they were never interested in him. They never came onto him. Until now. Henry pushed up his glasses, but they just slid back down his sweat-slick nose.

"Um, yeah, sounds good. But first, I gotta start some dinner, in case someone gets home."

"Okay."

Lana wandered through the house, eventually flipping on the TV. She stood there instead of sitting down, moving around restlessly, glancing into the kitchen every couple minutes to see what Henry was doing. Eventually, Henry went back to her.

"I can leave it for a while now."

"Guess we'll go in your bedroom, if your ma might get home."

"Yeah." Henry picked Bobby up and brought him into the room before shutting the door.

"Does he gotta be in the room?" Lana questioned, eying the baby as Henry put him down.

"I gotta keep an eye on him," Henry pointed out.

"Well, this'll be something new. I don't usually perform for an audience."

Lana was something else. Other girls were now unaccountably interested in him too, but Lana was at the forefront. She was the boldest, always ready to go with Henry to the mall, home, or wherever Henry was going. She wasn't happy if there was already another girl with Henry when she showed up. She said nothing, but her black expression said it all. She didn't like him seeing other girls, talking to them, or even just looking at them.

Then he suddenly started seeing her with another guy. She referred to Gus as her ex-boyfriend, but it was apparent to Henry that he was not so "ex."

He was disappointed at the sudden change in the situation, but he didn't pursue her. He wasn't the type. And there were other girls ready and willing to take her place. He just let her go.

That turned out to be a mistake.

———

When Lana saw that Henry wasn't going to challenge Gus for her, she tried playing it the other direction. Suddenly she was fawning all over Henry in front of Gus. And Gus didn't have Henry's laid-back personality.

Henry ran into Gus in a quiet hallway during third-period class. It was too late to retreat and go the other direction. Henry wasn't fast, and Gus was athletic, on both the football team and the wrestling team.

"Henry Thomas, isn't it?" Gus sneered.

"Yeah," Henry agreed, trying to squeeze past him without getting delayed.

"You think you're hot stuff with the girls now, don't you?" Gus demanded, moving squarely in front of Henry and forcing him to stop.

"No," Henry said firmly. The girls might think that, but he knew that he was the same nerdy, somewhat shy, but quick-talking kid that he'd always been. They'd known it then, and sooner or later, they would lose interest in him and he would go back to being beneath their notice.

"I'm warning you, kid—keep away from Lana," Gus growled.

"Why don't you tell her to keep away from me?" Henry countered.

Gus looked taken aback for a moment but then pressed on. "I'm telling both of you—I'd better not see you together again."

Henry shrugged. "Fine with me." He would miss Lana's

company, but it wasn't worth confronting Gus over. There were other girls. "She's all yours."

Gus eyed him, suspicious of his response. "What are you trying to pull? You're going to stay away from her."

"Yeah. But I can't control where she decides to show up," Henry warned.

"I'll take care of that."

They stood there for a moment, looking at each other. Henry raised an eyebrow, waiting. Gus shifted partly out of the way. "You'd better not be messing with me," he warned, just to get in the last word.

Henry slipped past him.

———

Henry didn't see Lana for a while, and he assumed that Gus had taken care of things. But after a few days of not seeing her, one of Lana's girlfriends passed him a note from her. She wanted to see Henry. Alone. At a specified time and place. Henry made sure the girl who had given him the note saw him flick it into the garbage. Henry turned back around and stared expressionlessly at the board.

He didn't show up at the rendezvous.

She didn't take the hint. A few days later, she showed up at his house after school. Her makeup didn't quite disguise her black eye.

Henry scowled. "What are you doing here?" he demanded.

"Didn't Marcia give you my note?"

"Yeah, she did," Henry said flatly.

"You didn't come see me."

"No."

"Why not?" she drew it out in a whine.

Henry looked her over in disbelief. Couldn't she take a hint? Did he have to come out and tell her bluntly?

"I was seeing someone else," he said.

"Someone else? What are you talking about?"

"I'm hanging with someone else now. A different girl."

"I don't care. See whoever you like. I don't care about being exclusive."

Henry shook his head. "You don't get it."

"What's to get?" she said stubbornly.

"I don't want to see you anymore."

Lana stared at him in disbelief, a red flush rising from her neck. "You don't *want* me?"

"No," Henry insisted. "I don't."

She took him by the hands, her gaze fiery and intense. "It's just Gus," she insisted. "He told you to say that. You care for me. I know you do. Gus won't do anything to you. He's just talk."

"It's not just Gus." That part was true. Henry didn't like Lana's scheming and jealousy. Girls like that were dangerous. He'd had enough experience with girls that caused trouble. "I'm just not interested in you."

That part was a lie.

Lana's eyes teared up and she turned away from him, shoulders shaking. Henry swallowed a lump swelling in his throat. It took all of his self-control to keep from calling her back. He watched her until she was out of sight. That would finally be the end of it.

But it wasn't.

23

Henry looked around him in confusion.

He was dreaming.

He had to be.

He was standing there in an orange jumpsuit. The boys around him were also in orange jumpsuits. They were all looking down at the floor where a couple of Corrections Officers lay bleeding. Or rather, one was bleeding, the other looked pretty dead.

There was a strange weight in Henry's arm, and he looked down and saw he was holding a gun. It fell to the floor with a clatter.

All the boys were looking around anxiously. A boy with dark, tangled hair looked directly at Henry and raised an eyebrow.

"Thanks, Specs," he acknowledged. "I woulda been a goner."

Henry tried to process what he was saying. "What?"

The boy gestured at the CO lying dead on the floor.

"I said thanks. Lucky thing you're a good shot."

"Did I kill him?" Henry said blankly.

"Oh yeah. He's dead as a doornail," the boy acknowledged.

"Hey, Marty," one of the other boys interrupted anxiously. "What now? What do we do now?"

Marty shrugged. He walked over to the computer terminal and clicked through a few screens. "It's locked down. We've got all the time in the world to figure out a game plan. This is the master lock. The CO's can't unlock anything unless I give them access from here."

Henry shifted uneasily. He looked the computer over. "It's networked," he pointed out, indicating the cables.

"Of course it is," Marty agreed. "How else is it going to control all of the electronic locks?"

"If it's networked, it means other people can get access. From inside, from outside, who knows?"

Marty contemplated this. "There'll be a firewall," he countered.

"Passwords. You have a password, you get through the firewall. Maybe backdoor passwords too; we can't tell how many."

One of the other boys pushed in front of Marty and sat down. He tapped away at the keyboard for a minute.

"That's the master," he said. "I changed the code. And I've locked out all the other users. That will stop an immediate assault. But he's right; the developer might have left a back door. Only a couple of people will know about it. It will take time to get a hold of anyone. We have some time to figure out what to do."

"What if you unplug the terminal?" Marty suggested.

"Other terminals might have access to the same functions. Server room too."

Henry sat down on the shabby couch nearby, studying it out in his mind. "We've got to get rid of all of the other termi-nals," he said. "Shut them down. From the server room right down to library computers. Disconnect every outside line. Leave this as the sole functioning terminal so that we control everything."

"Yeah. He's right," the boy at the computer agreed, still tapping away, figuring out what he could do from there.

Henry closed his eyes, feeling light-headed.

It had to be a dream. Nothing else made sense.

He would go back to sleep, and when he woke up, he would be back home, back in his real life instead of this dark, threatening dream world.

———

Henry awoke later to shouting. He shifted slowly, opening his eyes and glancing around. He didn't know how long he'd been asleep. His head was a little clearer this time, but the nightmarish feeling still hung over him.

He could remember more now. He could remember traveling to juvie in a van. Worrying about how he was going to get through his incarceration. He was a small, nerdy, naive kid. The kind of kid he knew would be preyed on in juvie. Juvie would be like one long gym class. Humiliating, bullied, no privacy, all the macho talk and jock stuff that goes on in the locker room.

That would be what juvie would be like for him.

There was another gap in Henry's memory after that. Somehow, he'd gotten mixed up with Marty and the others. And mixed up in the plot to take over the prison. The plot that was ultimately successful. And here he was, apparently with blood on his hands. Still helping them out, digging himself deeper. What had happened? How had he gotten involved with them? And what was he doing in juvie in the first place? None of it made any sense.

The shouting got louder. Or Henry was better able to focus on it, reaching through the fuzziness that enveloped his mind.

Azzi was yelling. Henry didn't recognize the other voice, but it was a deeper, fuller baritone. The voice of a man, not another juvenile. Henry glanced at the floor. The dead CO was still there, but the bleeding one was not. They must have removed him to another room, and he was now conscious, embroiled in some senseless yelling match with Azzi. The CO was used to being in control. Used to being able to tell the inmates what to do. He still figured if he yelled and bullied enough, he could still get his own way.

But Azzi was hollering back, and from the sound of things, hitting him and throwing things around. The CO was injured and presumably restrained. Shouting wasn't going to get him anywhere.

McNeil walked in and looked at Henry. "Hey, Sleeping Beauty," he greeted with a lazy grin. His smile was really quite stunning. There were high dental bills in his past. The girls would have said that he was gorgeous. But his equanimity amid a prison uprising could only mean one thing. Drugs. That, and the gun jutting casually out of his hip pocket, made him dangerous. Henry couldn't let himself be soothed into carelessness.

Henry rubbed at his sticky eyes. He was so dopey. He should get up. Do something. Force himself to be alert.

"I don't know how I could have fallen asleep," he said.

"It's cool. But you're missing the action."

Henry got to his feet, covering a wide yawn. "Yeah. What's —" He nearly tripped over the dead CO and had to find his footing again and go around. "What's going on?"

"Marty's making sure everything is secure. Azzi's interrogating our first prisoner. The rest of us are kicking around enjoying our first taste of freedom, stayin' out of Marty's way 'til he settles down."

"Freedom?" Henry repeated, looking around the small room. They were still in juvie, still in close quarters, with no hope of getting out.

McNeil shrugged. "It's freedom for us. You don't know. You ain't been here long enough to understand."

Henry accepted this. He didn't know how long he'd been

there. He couldn't remember being there at all before the uprising. "Where's the john?"

"I'll show you," McNeil offered, putting a friendly hand on Henry's shoulder.

Henry squirmed uncomfortably, trying to shrug it off.

"I'm just bein' friendly, don't get bent outta shape," McNeil growled.

Henry swallowed and put up with it. Upsetting McNeil would not be in his best interests.

———

Things moved slowly to Henry, like the whole world had been put in slow motion. Everything was so tense; Henry expected time to move faster, for the adrenaline to make him anxious and jumpy. But instead, he felt distanced, removed from everything that was going on around him.

"What's with the kid?" Henry heard one of the boys ask as he buried his face in his folded arms, and he knew 'the kid' meant him.

"It's the shock," Marty said. "He's traumatized, so his body shuts everything off 'til he gets over it. Happens to soldiers and hostages all the time. He'll get over it."

"I never did that when I—"

"Yeah, well, you ain't him, are you?" Marty growled. "You prob'ly seen your first body when you were two; how do you know how you acted? I mean, take a look at him. He's a naive kid, prob'ly never done a violent thing in his life. Suddenly he's in juvie, in the middle of this, with a gun in his hand and bodies on the floor."

"I guess."

"You guys gotta take it slow with him. Teach him the tricks of the trade. Talk slow. You know."

Thinking about what was happening, the voices got more and more distant, and the world gradually faded out again.

Henry was shaken awake. He rubbed his eyes drowsily, yawning. It was Azzi, a boy with a Middle Eastern look. Older than Henry.

"The boss says you ain't eaten in two days," Azzi said, shoving a plate with a sandwich on it under Henry's nose. "So, eat up. We need every man we got ready for action."

Henry sat up and balanced the plate on his lap. He obediently took a bite, though he had no appetite. His mouth was dry and he felt like he was eating glue. He glanced around for a drink. Anticipating, Azzi pushed a cup of coffee at him. It was lukewarm, but at least moistened the ball of glue in his mouth. Henry nodded his thanks.

Azzi stayed and watched him, apparently under orders to make sure he finished the sandwich.

"Sorry, there ain't nothing else," Azzi said, making small talk. "There's plenty in the mess, but we gotta find someone who can cook."

"I can cook," Henry offered before taking another bite.

"Yeah? Good. 'Cause the prisoners are gonna need to eat soon. We been feeding ourselves, but none of us felt like making a few hundred sandwiches."

"Where's the cook?"

"Locked down, like everyone else. Marty don't want no one with their hands on knives."

Henry shrugged. "Just take the knives out of the kitchen. Pretty much everything here is either warmed over or instant. I doubt they do anything in the kitchen but add water and heat stuff up."

Funny, he couldn't remember eating there before, but he knew that.

"Cool. I'll tell the boss. You're pretty handy for a nerd, aren't you?"

"I prefer geek," Henry said. It was a stock comeback for

him, but Azzi didn't run in his circles and thought it was hilarious. He laughed.

"You shoot, you know computers, you cook, and you're funny too! Man, I never met anyone like you before."

Henry laughed, shaking his head. Who knew he'd get popular in juvie? Not that they'd hated him at school, but none of them had really liked or admired him. He hadn't been popular. But Azzi acted like he was something special.

24

———————

Okay, gang, this is the score," Marty said sternly, once everyone had assembled. He walked down the short line of juvies. He'd had them all stand in a line, like soldiers, with their shoulders back and guts sucked in. He'd named his lieutenants briskly and informed the rest of them of their ranks. There might only be eight of them, but they were going to be strictly organized. That was what had gotten them where they were now.

"We've been locked down twenty-four hours. No doors have been opened. That means we got CO's locked in corridors with no idea what's going on. We gotta get them secured in cells, and we gotta disable any other computers to make sure we're secure."

"And release the other juvies," Daniel suggested.

"Shut up," Marty snapped angrily, turning to look at the boy. "Who's giving the orders here?"

Daniel pressed his lips together and looked straight ahead, stone-faced.

"We're not releasing the rest of the juvies. We do that, we lose control. Chaos. If we want to stay in control of things, we have to be careful who we release. One at a time and keeping strict discipline."

Everyone has careful not to look around at each other, but there was a feeling of discord that ran through the group. Marty would recognize that and keep it under control. He was right, of course. Henry could envision the pandemonium that would ensue if all the juvies were set free to overrun the prison. There would be no way to keep them all under control.

"Let's go," said Marty, pairing everybody off and instructing them what block to start in. Henry was paired up with McNeil. McNeil picked out weapons for each of them, handing a gun casually to Henry.

"I guess you know how to use it, all right. Just don't stand behind me."

Henry nodded. His mouth was dry. McNeil was a captain and Henry a private, so all he had to do was follow orders. McNeil was the one in charge of him.

They punched in the access code to open the first corridor door and were face-to-face with a CO. An angry guard who'd been locked in that hallway for twenty-four hours, between double rows of filled juvie cells. Without food, toilets, or privacy.

"What took so long?" he demanded as the door opened. Then he saw McNeil and Henry, and his eyes narrowed. "What's going on? What are you doing here?"

"Lace your hands behind your head," McNeil said politely, "or I'll blow your ugly head off."

"You can't tell me what to do!" the CO protested furiously, flushing a deep purple.

McNeil raised his gun, finger tightening on the trigger. Henry held his breath. McNeil and the guard stared at each other calculatingly for a couple of heartbeats.

Then McNeil pulled the trigger. Henry didn't know if he closed his eyes or blacked out, only that he didn't see the damage the bullet did. A cheer went up from the juvies in the cells.

Henry walked around the body on the floor. His feet stuck to the floor like in a movie theater. Then there were boos, catcalls, and angry swearing from the prisoners when they realized they weren't being released.

Henry and McNeil went through the next door. No CO in that corridor. The next CO they did run into had the sense to obey McNeil and was put into an empty cell without incident. The shouts coming from then locked up juvies was irritating. Henry pointed his gun at the noisiest boy.

"Shut up," he ordered tightly.

Everybody quieted. McNeil looked at Henry with an eyebrow raised, then shrugged. They moved on.

———

There was much celebration after all of the CO's were safely locked away and they were able to lift the general lock-down. Henry was sent down to the Mess with Daniel to rustle up a hot lunch. He looked through the lockers and cold room to see what he could make. Daniel watched him.

"So, what are you in for?" Daniel questioned.

Henry didn't answer right away. He thought about it. He couldn't remember what had brought him there. He could remember, though, the trouble with Liz. It was the only thing that they could have sent him to jail for. They must have decided it wasn't an accident after all and arrested him.

"Murder," he said casually, keeping his voice light and even. "A girl I knew."

"You?" Daniel challenged, sounding surprised. "You ain't the type."

Henry shrugged.

"You really did that?" Daniel persisted.

"She's really dead," Henry countered, not answering directly.

Daniel accepted this philosophically, nodding. "Yep. What was she—cheatin' on you?"

"She was sleepin' with everyone in the place."

"Yeah. Chicks. Can't trust any of them."

———

Marty plugged in the phone. He had unplugged it following the coup because it wouldn't stop ringing, and he wasn't ready to talk to the outside yet. Now, with the CO's secured and the computers taken care of, he was prepared to deal with the outside.

As soon as he picked up the receiver, he was in contact with the hostage negotiator.

"Hey. Who's this?" Marty demanded without preamble.

"I'm the police neg—"

"Yeah, I figured what you are; I want your name," Marty snapped.

"Oh, of course. My name is John Bab—"

"Okay, Johnny. What's your position on this?"

"What's your name?"

"Marty. What's the word?"

"Well, that depends," John said delicately. "What is the situation?"

"A few CO's dead," Marty said, unworried, "Couple injured. Plenty more locked up with the boys. We've got a core group of juvies running the place and the rest are still locked up."

"How big is your core group?" John inquired.

"Big enough to do what I need done and small enough to keep under control," Marty blustered, nodding at the boys who were listening with great interest to the conversation.

"Are you in command, then?"

"Yeah. So how hard are you going to make this?"

"We're not out to make this hard. But we do have a different outlook on this thing. What is it you're after?"

"Well, let's have a show of faith first. The boys are sick of the crap in Mess. They want pizza."

"Okay," the negotiator agreed.

"Call me when it arrives."

"What kind do you want?"

"Fifteen pizzas. Assorted toppings. Fifteen pop bottles. Mostly cola. No bugs or wires in the pizza boxes."

"I'll get onto it," he assured Marty.

"I'll expect your call in half an hour."

"It may take a little longer," Babcock warned.

"If it does, I'll know you're messing with the boxes. All the major chains deliver in thirty minutes. If one place can't make all fifteen, order from two places." Marty hung up the phone. He glanced around the room at the rest of the boys.

"Why fifteen?" Henry said.

Everybody looked at him like he was crazy. Marty frowned, his brows drawing down and his face flushing a little.

"Shut up, kid," Azzi muttered under his breath.

Henry could see no one understood his question. He wasn't sure if Marty did.

"Fifteen is too much for us," Henry said, "but not enough for the whole facility."

"That's right, Specs," Marty agreed. "They know that it's not enough for everyone, so they'll think we have a larger force in control."

Everyone nodded, impressed with Marty's genius. Marty walked over and patted Henry on the back.

"You're a smart kid. Keep your eyes open."

Henry nodded. "I will."

25

Henry awoke from the dream and stared into the darkness, panicked. His heart raced out of control.

He could remember.

More than he wanted to remember. He wished he could go back to the blankness that had previously enveloped his mind. Just push it all out and wrap the darkness of forgetfulness around him again. It was better not remembering.

Lana was dead. They said it was an accidental drug overdose. Henry knew she used.

But then they changed the story to suicide, for a day or two. Henry didn't know much about what had happened, what evidence they might have.

Then after another day or so, the cops were knocking on his door. Before long, they had enough evidence to arrest him for her murder.

Murder.

Henry was sure it must have been suicide. The breakup… Henry had seen how emotional she was when she left. She wouldn't have taken that big an overdose by accident. She'd been distraught. But Lana's girlfriends had told the cops how she'd been playing the boys against each other.

And the cops had looked Henry up and found out about Liz. With a previous suspicious death on his sheet, they liked Henry for Lana's murder.

———

Liz and Lana. Lana and Liz.

How did he manage to get mixed up with both of them?

He didn't do anything wrong. He would never harm another person intentionally, let alone kill her.

"Hey, Specs."

Henry jumped and looked around quickly. It was Marty, of course, watching him quizzically.

"You're talking in your sleep," Marty said.

"I wasn't asleep," Henry objected.

"I know… that's what makes it weird," Marty said, one eyebrow cocked.

Henry shifted uncomfortably. "I was… just talking to myself. I forgot there was anyone else around," Henry explained awkwardly.

"Are you supposed to be on meds?" Marty questioned. "Lots of guys are, you know. Don't sweat it."

"No. I was just talking to myself."

"Okay. It's your turn on watch. You're with McNeil. Do what he tells you."

Henry nodded. He turned to go. "McNeil… gives me the creeps," he ventured, stopping in the doorway. "Is he… okay?"

"If he was okay, he wouldn't be here. We all got our problems," Marty said philosophically. "They don't send you here just because they don't like your face."

"I guess. But maybe," Henry stumbled, "maybe you don't put us together on night duty too much."

Marty's expression darkened. "I like you, kid, so I'll overlook insubordination once," he said sternly, "but only once. You don't question my commands."

"I wasn't questioning—" Henry tried to backtrack.

"McNeil likes you. I wanna keep him happy. So you'll go on night watch together however often I tell you to."

Henry nodded and walked out. He didn't like it, but he could see that Marty wasn't going to help him out

He'd have to look after himself.

Henry looked half-heartedly for something to use as a weapon. He knew it was ridiculous to be looking for a knife when he and McNeil both had guns already. But it was juvie, and in juvie, they used knives.

That was just the way it was done.

———

Henry walked briskly down the corridor. Most of the juvies appeared to be sleeping. They were used to being locked up and knew that staying awake would only make time pass more slowly. The CO's, though, were a different story. They were mostly still awake—pacing, watching each other, making a fuss when Henry walked by. Henry walked by as fast as he could.

One of the CO's was watching him through the bars, standing right at the front of the cell.

"Kid… kid…" the man called, trying to get him to go closer.

Henry was careful not to get close enough to be grabbed. But something in his voice made Henry slow down.

"You gotta help us, kid. Come on."

"I can't do anything," Henry murmured.

"You don't know what it's like, here," his voice was desperate. "They keep putting stuff in my food. I can't sleep, I'm going crazy in here."

Henry looked at his wide, wild eyes and could not find anything to say or to continue on his patrol.

"You're not like the others," the CO pleaded. "You're a decent guy. You know no one deserves to be treated like this.

We didn't treat prisoners this way. We were decent. We didn't foul your food. You got out for exercise and socializing. This is torture. You can do something about it. Help us. Help me."

Henry took a hesitant step towards him. The man really was in pain.

"Step back, soldier," a voice commanded lazily.

Henry recognized McNeil's voice and stepped back as sharply as if jolted by an electric shock.

McNeil walked up behind him and stood there in silence for a moment, standing way too close for comfort. Henry could feel McNeil's breath on his neck.

"This man is trying to deceive you," McNeil whispered. "He is trying to get you to betray your brothers in arms."

Henry hated all of their army talk. They weren't in an army and they weren't fighting for the greater good.

They were juvies holding hostages—law-abiding hostages who didn't deserve to be mistreated.

"Yes, sir," he said, careful to keep his voice calm.

"Do you know why he's talking to you? Because he knows you weren't here long enough to learn the ropes. To know the good CO's from the bad."

The CO's face grew angry and red. He was transformed before Henry's eyes from a desperate hostage to an angry, vengeful prisoner.

"You seen anyone mess with his food? You make it yourself; half the time, you take it around yourself. No one has a chance to contaminate it. It's his own idea—because he's done it to us." McNeil shook his head sadly. "Why do you think we're doing this? Because we were bored? Felt like some pizza? Or because we think we can get a rich ransom off it? Come on, kid. We get enough attention; we can get conditions changed around here. That's all we're trying to do."

Henry nodded. "I didn't know."

"When you're patrolling along here," McNeil gestured to the CO, "night or day—you don't look in their eyes. You don't talk to them. You don't listen to a word they say. You're behind a wall. You're separate."

"Okay."

McNeil put his arm around Henry's shoulders. "You can't afford to be soft in here, kid. You can't let yourself be taken in by these guys."

Henry's skin crawled.

"I get it," he said.

"Good. Let's get out of here. Too many rats around here."

26

Henry was starting to remember the last couple of days before the coup at juvie. He hadn't been there very long. He was still very green. And scared. For some reason, they had bunked him with Marty and two of his boys.

Henry was very careful, not wanting to upset anyone or breach any unwritten rules.

"Uh—which bunk isn't taken?" he had asked hesitantly, gesturing at them.

"Can't you see we're having an important discussion?" Freeman demanded.

Henry ducked his head and withdrew. Marty turned and looked him over.

"You bunk with me," he said, motioning to the beds on the left. "Top, bottom, I don't care which."

"Thanks."

Henry climbed onto the upper bunk and lay down, his back to them. He was so scared about what was going to happen.

Was the reason that Marty didn't care where he slept because he would try to take advantage of him no matter which bed he chose?

Was it a test? Did he just want a reason to beat Henry up?

Despite his concerns, he started to drift into unconsciousness. The other boys began talking again after a decent interval to make sure that Henry was asleep. A word here and there pierced Henry's conscience.

Words like guns and coup. Words like fight and hostage and bloodshed.

Henry tried to burrow deeper into his dreams.

After lights out, somebody reached up into Henry's bunk and grabbed his arm. His grip was as hard as steel. Henry gasped loudly and rolled over to protect himself.

"You wanna know what we do with greenies around here?" Freeman questioned.

Henry tried to swallow, but his mouth and throat were too dry.

"Don't—" he croaked in protest.

"You been listening to our business," Freeman growled, "and I don't like snitches."

"No," Henry protested.

Freeman pulled him down from the bed with a crash. Henry cowered, unsure where or how to protect himself.

"Leave the kid be," Marty ordered. "You're scarin' the daylights outta him. You ain't gonna cause us any trouble, are you, kid?"

"No," Henry insisted. "I won't. I swear."

"You see? He's on our side."

"Aw, let me have some fun with 'im, Marty," Freeman questioned in good humor. "Newbies are such a kick, and look how fresh he is."

Marty didn't answer right away. Henry breathed shallowly, curled up tightly in a ball, praying for protection. Marty chuckled lowly.

"Leave 'im be, Freeman. We can't afford to attract attention right now."

"I won't leave a mark; promise," Freeman wheedled.

"Next time."

Freeman sighed and got into his own bunk. Henry didn't budge from his spot on the floor.

"Get up, kid," Marty said. "You'll have the heat on us, lying there like that."

Henry weakly got to his feet. He tried unsuccessfully to pull himself up into the top bunk. After a few attempts, Marty intervened.

"Take the bottom. I'll take the top."

"Thanks," Henry whispered gratefully, and climbed in even before Marty finished crawling out.

—

The first morning in juvie, Henry had said he was sick. They had let him stay in bed instead of forcing him to shower and eat with the others. Henry just snuggled under the covers and tried to avoid thinking about the mess he was in.

He wondered who was looking after Bobby, but put it out of his mind. There was no point in worrying about it. There was nothing he could do.

His ears were soon filled with the plotting of Marty and his boys again. Hushed, urgent tones, but loud enough for Henry to make out their words. He didn't know all of the details, but he knew enough.

And it wouldn't be long before they put a gun in his hand and made him a part of it.

27

———————

Henry stared at the phone. He was the only one around. The others were sleeping, or on watch, or otherwise engaged. He thought that he could do something. Something to resolve the situation. Henry was smart. He could do it.

Finally, Henry picked up the phone, his fingers slippery with sweat. "Hello?" his own voice sounded small on the line.

"Who's this?" John, the hostage negotiator, questioned.

Henry cleared his throat and tried to speak more confidently. "My name is Henry."

"Hi, Henry," John said warmly. "So, what's up?"

"I—I want to help."

"Do you think you can help me? I'd sure appreciate any help you could provide."

Henry nodded, his voice failing. John let the silence lengthen for a minute before speaking.

"Are you still there, Henry?"

"Yeah."

"Are you alone?"

"Yeah."

"How many guys are there in there? How many free, in Martin's 'core group'?"

"About ten so far."

"What can you tell me about the set-up?"

Henry considered. He figured they probably already knew everything that he could tell them. He didn't know enough of the details of the changing watches and security measures to be of any help.

"I—not really anything. I'm just... nobody. Got stuck in the middle. What about—what about the computer?"

"The system?" Henry could hear papers rifling in the background. Muffled voices. "Do you think you can help us with the electronics, Henry?"

"Maybe. I might be able to plug the outside line back in."

"That might be helpful."

"Is there a backdoor?" Henry questioned.

"Backdoor?" John repeated, and Henry could hear more voices and papers in the background. Henry hung up the phone quickly. He had barely done so when Azzi walked into the room. Henry breathed a sigh of relief. His heart pounded so fast he could hardly breathe. He was sure Azzi would notice how he was sweating. His face burned and he was sure he must be flushed.

"Hey," Azzi greeted. He didn't appear to notice anything suspicious.

"Hi."

"I think Marty was lookin' for you to get lunch ready or something."

"Okay. I'll go see what he wants."

Henry tried to calm himself as he went to find Marty. Marty would see through him. Marty would know that he was up to something. He was too good at reading people not to know. Henry found Marty in the main control room. Henry glanced at the main computer, flushing guiltily. He suddenly really needed to use the toilet.

"Hey, Specs. Anything good down in Mess?" Marty inquired.

"What do you want?"

"Burgers and fries."

Henry frowned, thinking about it. "Well, I'll see what I can do."

"Thanks."

———

Henry puttered around the kitchen, trying to think about the cooking. He tried to block out the phone call, the computer, and everything but making dinner. He had to block it out, keep his mind separated from everything else.

After a while, Marty came down the stairs into the kitchen, sniffing the air. "Something sure smells good down here! What're you making?"

"I disassembled a couple of frozen dinners to take out the beef and put'em in a bun," Henry explained. "I can make'em like sloppy joes or beef dip, or put ketchup on them. And I took some scalloped potatoes without the sauce and I'm roasting them in the oven. I can put ketchup or gravy or whatever you want on them."

"You're a genius, kid. When we get put back behind bars, I want you to stay on as my personal cook. Maybe I'll make it one of my demands, huh?"

Henry tried to smile, but he knew it was a stretch. Marty chuckled.

"You gotta laugh at yourself sometimes, kid."

"Sorry, I'm wound pretty tight," Henry acknowledged.

"Azzi says you got a good sense of humor. How come you never joke around me?"

"I guess because I'm scared of you," Henry answered honestly.

Marty laughed. "There you go. So how long before this is ready?"

"Just a few minutes. How do you want the bun and fries?"

"Ketchup on the bun, gravy on the fries."

His ears were soon filled with the plotting of Marty and his boys again.

28

Marty was tied up for a few minutes eating in the kitchen, so Henry went back to the main control room. Sweating, he looked around to make sure no one was close by. He plugged the cord back into the back of the computer, and it snapped back into place with a loud click. Henry watched the screen. Nothing happened. Would he be able to tell if someone was accessing it? Would others? Henry loosened the connection on the back of the monitor until the screen went blank. He got back up and left the room.

Henry wondered if all of the phones were rigged to go directly to John. He couldn't get to the main phone that he and Marty had previously used. There were too many people around. Eventually, he couldn't stand it any longer and he went to one of the other offices. He didn't turn the light on. He didn't want to attract any attention. He picked up the phone and crawled under the desk where he couldn't be seen. He pulled his sweat-soaked uniform away from his body and picked up the phone.

"Hello?"

"Hi," it was John.

"It's Henry," he told John.

"That's what I thought. How are things going in there, Henry?"

"I plugged the computer phone line in. Did you find out if there's a back door?"

"I'm told that there is. But we need some more details from you. We can't just perform a lock-down. Then our guys can't get in."

"Yeah, okay."

"So tell me, Henry, what's your motivation behind all of this?"

Henry considered his answer before answering. "I shouldn't even be here, you know. I know everyone says it. But they don't even have any evidence against me."

"Are you saying you'll help if you're promised a free release?"

Henry shook his head, bumping it on the desk. When had he asked for anything in return for help? "No—I just want someone to take another look at my case."

"You were convicted without evidence?"

"I haven't been convicted of anything. I haven't gone to trial."

"I see."

"Don't you have access to everyone's records?" Henry quizzed, frowning.

"Well, we haven't had access to the computer, so we've had to do everything manually. And believe it or not, you're not the only Henry in there."

"Oh. It's sort of a geeky name. I haven't run into any others."

"Yeah, they usually have weird nicknames. You never had a nickname?"

"None I liked, no," Henry said, with a slight laugh. He'd been called a lot of things. But he'd never actually gone by anything other than Henry.

"So where are you situated, Henry? What room are you in?" John questioned.

"I don't know the number. It's an office in the main wing."

"And where are the others?"

"Marty's in the mess, unless he's finished eating already. One or two will be patrolling the cells. Everyone else will just be hanging out, playing cards or whatever."

"Are they all fairly centralized?"

"Yeah. All in the main wing, except for Marty and the guards."

"Okay. The first thing we're going to do is lock out anyone not in the main wing. That will hopefully isolate your leader and a couple of guns. After that, we'll have to act fast, before anyone realizes we have control over the computer."

"Yeah, okay."

"I want you to think carefully. You said there were about ten of you free. Is that accurate?"

"Yeah."

"Including Marty?"

"Yeah."

"And you?"

"Yeah."

"So if you're on our side, and we've isolated Marty and two others, that only leaves half a dozen to contend with."

"Right."

There were urgent voices in the background.

"Okay. This is all going to happen pretty fast," John warned. "Are you armed?"

Henry felt his waistband. He was still carrying a gun.

"Uh—yeah."

"Okay. I want you to put it on the floor and kick it away."

Henry did. "Okay."

"Is it a good distance away? You don't want to make our SWAT team nervous."

"Yeah, it's out of reach," Henry reassured him.

"They're going to be using tear gas. I don't want you to panic. In just a minute, I want you to put down the phone and lie on your stomach with your hands behind your head. If you keep down on the floor and close your eyes, the tear gas won't bother you as much."

"Okay."

There was a long silence from John. Henry could hear a chaos of background noises but couldn't differentiate between them. Then he heard John's voice again.

"Okay, get ready. Put down the phone and lie flat."

Henry's stomach twisted. His shirt was sticking to him again. He put down the phone and lay down. At first, nothing happened. Then he heard the clank of doors opening. There was dead silence and then shouting and yelling. Henry braced for shots, but heard none. The tear gas started to seep into the room. Henry shut his eyes tightly and tried not to breathe the gas any more than possible. The shouting quieted and there were opening and closing doors. It was a few minutes before Henry realized they were looking for him. They were a couple of doors away still. Henry raised his head for a moment, but the gas stung his eyes and he put it down again. Then the door flew open and booted feet rushed in.

"Here he is!" a deep voice shouted. Henry started to rise, only to be kicked back to the floor.

"Don't move! Hands behind your head!"

"But—" Henry tried to protest, to tell them that he was one of the good guys. But they weren't listening.

"Stay still!"

Henry was kicked again. Rough hands wrenched his arms around behind his back and cuffed them. They raised him to his feet, and Henry coughed and choked in the clouds of gas. His eyes blurred with tears.

He was hustled out to the compound outside and thrown to the ground. The others were there too. He could hear Azzi cursing, one of the others crying, everyone sniffling and coughing from the tear gas. There was muttering and grumbling about the bust, but no one was shouting slogans and 'never surrender.'

They weren't real terrorists. They were a group of juvies who got lucky and who always knew that sooner later, they'd get caught and be prisoners again.

Henry was quickly frisked, strong hands firmly groping for hidden weapons. Then they lifted him to his feet and escorted him to a dark-colored car, pushing him in so clumsily that he knocked his head on the roof before sliding into his seat.

Tears were still running down his cheeks. Henry kept blinking, trying to clear them. He hadn't even had that much exposure to the gas. They eventually pulled up to a police station, which Henry could now see. It was blurry even though the tears had stopped, but it wasn't until Henry tried to use his shoulder to readjust his glasses that he realized he'd lost them in the fracas. He let the cop who'd driven him lead him into the station and walk him into an interrogation room. Henry sat down at the table. Another man came in and sat across from him. Henry squinted at him, his eyes burning still.

"Hello, Henry," he greeted.

Henry thought he recognized the voice. "John?"

"Yeah. How are you doing?"

"I lost my glasses."

"We'll see what we can do about that. I want to thank you for your help in getting the prison under our control again."

Henry nodded. "No one was hurt?"

"No. Not during the operation. During the uprising—well, you know as well as anyone."

"Yeah. It all happened so fast. I didn't know what was going on."

"Exactly how did you get mixed up in it?"

"I was in Marty's cell. I didn't have anything to do with it; I was just caught in the middle of everything."

"I see. Well, make yourself comfortable. I expect you'll be here for a while until things are sorted out."

"And then what?"

"I don't know, kid. It all depends on your record, witness testimony, that sort of thing."

"Can I call my family?"

"No," John said flatly.

"I don't get a phone call?"

"I'll let you know later. Right now, you're part of a terrorist group and we can hold you for a while without allowing you communication with the outside."

Henry frowned, wondering if that was really the truth. It didn't sound right to him. But then, he'd never been part of a terrorist group before.

29

John left Henry by himself.

Time seemed to stand still. He sat there, waiting in the cold, silent room. He wondered if the others were being told that he turned on them. He wondered about Dorry and Bobby. His body started to ache. He could feel the bruises from being manhandled in the bust.

He had that curious feeling of wanting to sleep again. Just to shut off and withdraw into himself. He studied the bare room, the scarred table, the light fixture, his hands, trying to stay alert and aware. But the desire to sleep was overwhelming. Henry eventually put his head down on the table and closed his eyes, just for a minute.

He didn't know how much time had passed before another cop came in. He knew by the man's shape and clothing that it was not John, but couldn't make out his face. The cop pulled out a chair and sat down.

"Tell me about yourself, Henry," he suggested.

Henry rubbed his eyes. "What about me?" he questioned.

"You were in juvie for murder."

"No. I wasn't convicted. Just waiting for trial," Henry explained.

"What happened?"

"A girl I knew OD'd. They thought maybe I injected her or something. There's no evidence, though; you just look at my file."

"Why would they think you killed her if there was no evidence?"

"She was sort of my girlfriend for a while."

Funny, he had never actually thought of Lana as a girlfriend. They hung around together, messed around, but there were other girls too, and she had other guys. They weren't exclusive boyfriend-girlfriend, but what else would he call that?

"We broke up and she overdosed. I don't know. I guess they thought I was upset about the breakup."

"Were you?"

"I was more upset about her dying."

"Sure. Why did you break up?"

Henry shifted uncomfortably. "Why don't you read my file?"

"You wanted us to look into the case again. That was one of the reasons that you helped get us into juvie, right? So cooperate or I'm not going to waste my time on it." His voice was tough, stern.

"Lana had this old boyfriend that she got back together with again. She was still hanging out with me, too. He said shove off and I shoved off." Henry gave a helpless shrug.

"So, someone else muscled in on your girl."

"Yeah."

"And you weren't mad about it."

"If I was mad, wouldn't I go after him, not her?" Henry pointed out. "If I kill her, what do I get out of it?"

"If you can't have her, no one can," the man suggested.

"I didn't kill her. I'm not that kind of person."

"You've been under investigation for murder before," the man countered.

"That was an accident." Henry kept his voice even. "Not murder."

"It looked enough like an accident that they figured they couldn't win a jury. That doesn't mean you didn't do it."

"I never killed anyone. Never."

"Why didn't you fight for this Lana?" He jumped back to the earlier line of questioning.

"I didn't think it was worth it. And this other guy was really cut, you know? A guy like me is no match for him."

"So, you got back at him by taking her away from him."

"I didn't kill Lana," Henry growled, frustrated. "You think I wanted to go through all of this?"

"Of course not. No one ever thinks they're going to be caught."

"If I was going to kill her, I'd make it look like an accident. Isn't that what you think?"

"You're a smart kid. You thought it through. Varied your method."

Henry scowled. "Where's the evidence? You got no evidence that points to me. You can't arrest every guy whose ex-girlfriend dies."

"You've had an interesting history."

Henry was thrown. "What are you talking about?"

"Well, there's the other girl that died. There's the dead hamster thing before that. There's shoplifting—"

Henry's face heated with embarrassment. He rubbed the bridge of his nose where his glasses should have been. "I made a mistake," he protested. "It was an accident."

"You try to walk out of the store with a two-hundred-dollar music player? I'll say you made a mistake," the interrogator said with amusement.

"I just forgot I was holding onto it. What's that got to do with Lana?" Henry tried to divert his interrogator's attention away from the one thing they really did have on Henry.

"It shows a pattern of law-breaking. It shows that you have

little regard for the rules of society. And the hamster shows you have no regard for life. Those are dangerous patterns. You add this little bit of trouble in juvie and the guards that were killed, and that tells me you're well over the line. You're a cowardly, cold-blooded killer."

"The only thing you've got on me is shoplifting," Henry said reasonably. "Not Lana and Liz, not the hamster, and not the guards at juvie." He felt his temperature rising and tried to hold back a wave of emotion. "You ask any of the guys who were there. I had nothing to do with the uprising." He hoped he was right about the others not admitting who'd pulled the trigger on whom. That was the code, wasn't it? Besides, who'd believe that he had pulled the trigger and not Marty? They couldn't prove it.

"You had a gun on you."

"I didn't use it. We all had to have guns when we patrolled. Orders from Marty."

"Yours was missing bullets."

Henry gulped. "We just grabbed whatever was handy," he explained. "We didn't have the same ones all the time."

"Yours killed a guard."

"We didn't use the same guns all the time," Henry repeated with more emphasis.

"You have an answer for everything, hey?"

"I'm innocent," Henry said.

"Oh, don't try the naive and innocent kid act on me. I know more about you than anyone else."

Henry swallowed and wiped at the sweat beading along his hairline. "I want a lawyer. I want to talk to someone. I'm not answering any more questions."

"You wanted a new investigation."

"It wasn't a condition of my helping. Just a request, when John asked what I wanted. You're not listening any more than the other cops!"

"That's because the facts are the same. The facts don't change."

"Please let me call my family." Henry's voice cracked and changing pitch.

The cop stared at him without saying anything. Eventually, he stood up and walked out. Henry was left alone again.

———

The next time the door opened, a cop was there with a figure that Henry recognized, even without his glasses.

"Clint," he said with relief; and then when Dorry didn't follow him into the room. "Where's Ma?"

"She couldn't come, Sport."

Clint came closer and put something on the table. Henry looked down.

"They told me you broke your glasses," Clint explained. He'd brought Henry's spare pair.

Henry gratefully picked them up and put them on. Tears started in his eyes at the small act of kindness. "Is Ma at home?" he questioned roughly.

Clint cleared his throat, glancing at the officer, who Henry now saw was a large-jowled, red-cheeked man with watery blue eyes.

"No. She was having some problems," he explained. "She's at the clinic."

Henry wasn't surprised. "Bobby?" he questioned. "Who's looking after him?"

"Someone else is looking after him for a while."

"Social Services?" Henry dropped his voice.

"No, just one of the moms she knows from the playgroup."

"Oh, okay." Henry nodded, relieved.

"What do you need, Hank?" Clint questioned. "I don't know what I'm supposed to do here."

Henry looked at the officer for guidance. "What now?" he questioned.

"We're finished with the questioning for today. They're just figuring out where everyone's being transferred to. We don't exactly want to put all these boys back together again," he confided to Clint with a chuckle.

"So, he's not coming home?" Clint questioned.

The cop laughed. "Why would he go home?"

"They arrested another guy for that girl's murder," Clint said, as if everyone knew that.

"Who?" Henry asked, startled.

"That other boy she was seeing."

"Gus?"

Clint shrugged.

Henry looked at the cop. "They can't arrest two people for the same murder."

"Of course they can. And I can't do anything about it. You have to talk to the officers investigating it."

"You gotta get me a lawyer to talk to them," Henry told Clint. "Just call legal aid."

"What about the one you had when they arrested you?"

"I dunno what happened to him. But he was no good anyway."

"Okay. I'll call them and get someone else."

"Are you his guardian?" the cop questioned Clint.

"No. He's just got his ma."

"We're going to need to inform her about the new charges relating to the prison uprising."

"New charges?" Henry repeated. "I didn't do anything!"

"You were one of the conspirators," he pointed out. "You're not going to get away without any charges."

"His mom can't come." Clint said.

"I guess we'll need a hearing to put him in care of Family Services."

Henry's stomach twisted. In care of Family Services. He couldn't be in foster care again. But he wouldn't be in foster care. He'd be in juvie. He wasn't sure what the penalty for prison breaking was, but it wouldn't be short.

"Don't worry, Sport," Clint said, seeing his panic. "The lawyer will straighten it all out. Another day or two, you'll be back home. They can't keep you in jail without evidence."

Henry nodded, a lump in his throat. "Will you be seeing Bobby and Ma?"

"Sure."

"Tell them hi for me…?"

"Yeah, of course. And you'll see them soon."

"Okay."

Clint patted him awkwardly on the shoulder and nodded a wordless goodbye, shrugging embarrassedly. Clint didn't handle shows of emotion well.

30

Henry sat on a bench, waiting. He had a plastic bag at his feet with his few possessions in it. The time crept by. There was a clock on the wall and the hands crawled so slowly he thought it would start going backward.

At last, Clint came in. He nodded at Henry.

"Hey, kid."

He went up to the desk and signed some papers to get Henry released. He motioned to Henry to follow when he was done, and Henry walked with him out to the car.

"Bet you're glad to get out of there," Clint commented.

"Yeah. I can't believe I'm finally going home. It seems like forever."

Neither had anything else to say most of the way home. Henry stared out the window, thinking and reflecting over the chaos of the past few weeks. The silence between him and Clint was awkward. Clint was not a talkative man, and he and Henry didn't really have a close relationship. They dealt with each other because they lived in the same house, but there was no father-son bond. Not like with Frank. No one was like Frank.

"Is Ma home yet?" Henry questioned.

"No. She's still at the clinic. But once you've been home for a bit, she'll be back."

"And Bobby?"

"I got the address. You can go get him."

"Okay."

They were silent again. They got out of the car at the house. When they got in, Clint spoke without turning around.

"The address is by the phone."

Henry put his bag in his bedroom. He went to the kitchen and looked at the pad beside the phone. There was a scribbled phone number and address by the name 'Bobby.' There was also a number with 'Marty' beside it that made Henry frown. He ignored it for the moment and called the number by Bobby's name.

"Hi, it's Henry Thomas. Bobby's brother."

"Oh, hi. You're home," the woman's voice was cautious.

"Yeah. Is it okay if I come by for Bobby?"

"I guess. Right now?"

"Yeah."

"Okay… I'll get his things together."

Henry hung up and walked over there. He knocked and let himself in. The woman from the playgroup walked out from the back hall.

"I guess you're Henry. I'm Cheryl."

"Hi."

He half-waved, not knowing if he should shake her hand or something. Bobby toddled out from the hallway behind her.

"He's walking," Henry said in surprise.

"Yes, for about a week. Pretty unsteady still."

Bobby looked at Henry without recognition. He held onto Cheryl's leg and hid his face shyly. Henry's heart sank.

"He doesn't know me," he said.

"Give him a little bit of time," Cheryl advised. "A few weeks is a long time for a baby. He'll figure out who you are after a while."

She seemed jumpy, nervous about him, like he might grab Bobby and haul him out kicking and screaming.

"Can I hang out here for a bit? Until he's ready?" Henry asked.

"Sure." She smiled. They sat down in the living room. "So is your mom back home?"

"No, but probably she'll be back soon. She... kind of depends on me. Once she knows I'm home, she'll be back."

There was silence for a moment. Cheryl was awkward.

"She always talks very highly about you. She says that you're really smart and responsible. Really good with Bobby."

Henry shrugged. It might all be true, but he didn't feel very good about himself these days. The compliment was empty. Henry watched Bobby still hiding behind Cheryl.

"Hey, Squirt. How are you doing? You want to come home?"

Bobby sucked on his finger, watching Henry intently with big eyes.

"We'll go for a walk. Maybe stop at the park, at the slide. You'd like to go on the slide, huh?"

Bobby wasn't sure.

"Has he eaten?" Henry questioned, just filling the silence.

"He had some macaroni for lunch. Probably be hungry again around four, after his afternoon nap."

"Yeah. He wakes up hungry," Henry agreed. "How long have you been looking after him?"

"A couple weeks."

"Sorry about that. This business at juvie... some things are out of your control, you know?"

"I guess so. People can be falsely accused, even convicted..." she trailed off and shrugged.

"Yeah."

Bobby leaned forward, looking at Henry intently. Henry winked. Bobby looked surprised. He reached towards Henry.

"Ha!"

Henry grinned. "Yeah. You know me now? You remember Henry?"

"Ha-ry." Bobby reached out both pudgy arms. Henry took Bobby in his arms and cuddled him. Bobby crowed and patted Henry's cheek happily, singing, "Ha, Ha, Ha!" excitedly at the top of his voice.

Cheryl smiled. "There you go. Now he remembers."

"Yeah. That's better."

Henry gathered up Bobby's things, said a couple more good-byes and thank-yous to Cheryl, and took Bobby home.

———

Henry had just finished putting Bobby down to bed the next evening when Clint got home.

"Hey, Clint?" he called, going into the kitchen to meet him.

"What?" Clint snapped.

Great. Henry took a step back and shifted his weight, trying to decide what to do. Clint was drunk, and Henry did his best to have nothing to do with Clint when he was drunk.

"What do you want?" Clint demanded.

"I just… I just wondered about the note by the phone. Marty. Is that someone Mom's supposed to call?"

Looking in the fridge, Clint shook his head.

"No. That's for you. Some kid from school or something. He said call between two and four." Clint settled on a beer and closed the fridge. "Is that it?"

"Yeah. Thanks."

Henry retreated to his room and shut the door. He lay down on the bed, staring up at the ceiling. Marty. Between two and four. Visiting hours at juvie. How did Marty get his number, and what did he want from Henry?

31

Henry didn't call Marty back for a few days, but eventually, he had to. It was bothering him too much. He had a deep, aching dread in the pit of his stomach all the time, and he couldn't distract himself, or sleep or eat to make it go away.

Clint wasn't home during the day, and Dorry wasn't back from the clinic yet. Henry waited until Bobby went to sleep for his afternoon nap and then summoned up the courage to pick up the phone and dial. A gruff guard answered.

"Juvenile detention," he snapped.

"I… I need to talk to one of the inmates," Henry stammered nervously.

"Which one?"

"Umm, John Martin."

"What's your name?"

"Joe," Henry lied.

"Joe what?" the guard demanded.

"Uh—Johnson," Henry offered, his voice cracking.

"Try your real name now," the man suggested, sounding almost bored.

For a minute, Henry couldn't say anything. He considered

whether he should just hang up the phone. He hadn't thought about them taking his name down when he called. He didn't really want to be on the record as having called Marty.

"Henry Thomas," he admitted finally, with a small sigh of defeat.

"Hold the line," the guard directed.

Henry swallowed and waited. It was a long, anxious wait. It was nearly half an hour before the line was picked up again, and Henry had started to consider just hanging up. No one was going to answer. They'd forgotten him. Then there was a click on the line and then Marty's voice. Laconic, friendly.

"Hey, Specs. I was starting to wonder if the rumor you got out was wrong!"

Henry didn't know what to say about that. He cleared his throat uncomfortably. "How'd you know?" he asked stiffly.

"Prison grapevine's faster than the six o'clock news. How'd you get released?"

"Someone else confessed to the murder I was arrested for."

"That was lucky. And they didn't hold you responsible for your part in the coup?" Marty pressed.

"I got a good lawyer, clean record, told them I didn't take part..." Henry trailed off.

"And you had co-operated with them regaining control," Marty finished for him.

Henry stopped breathing. He couldn't think of what to say. He didn't know how Marty could possibly know. Or was it just a bluff?

Marty's low chuckle came down the line. "Who else would it be?" he questioned. "You think I don't know my own men? I'd been locked in a cell with most of them for more than a year. I know how they're going to respond. And I know how a naive kid who's never been up the river is going to respond too."

"I'm—sorry," Henry apologized. His heart was pounding and his face flushed with heat. Anyone looking at him now would know that he was guilty. He tried to slow his breathing down and pulled his shirt away from his body.

"No sweat," Marty said breezily. "We got what we set out to get. An investigation into the conditions in juvie and a transfer out of there."

"But you're somewhere worse—higher security."

"Higher security ain't always worse. They keep in line, follow the rules. Not like before," Marty explained.

Henry had only gotten a sense of what things had been like in juvie before he got there from the comments other boys had made. CO's who abused the boys. Administrative 'mistakes.' Fouled food.

"Oh," Henry said lamely. "Well, good."

"So, you wanna know what I called you for?" Marty teased.

"Yeah, I guess."

"I need someone on the outside to do some things for me."

"I can't do anything…" Henry protested.

"Nothin' big, Specs. Just a few little errands."

Henry started to argue and Marty cut him off. "You want me to change my story," Marty challenged him, "and tell them which one of my boys killed that CO?"

"No," Henry said quickly. He gulped and set his jaw, nodding slightly, steeling himself. "I'll do what you want."

———

Henry was nervous driving the car. He had a learner's license, but he wasn't supposed to be driving by himself. And Bobby was in a seatbelt when he should be in a baby seat. There'd be trouble if anyone saw him. He parked at the far end of the parking lot where he didn't have to worry about accidentally dinging other cars. After unbuckling Bobby, he walked to the admitting entrance. There was a line-up. He tried to keep Bobby entertained while they waited.

"I'm here to pick up my Mom," he told the receptionist once he got to the front of the line. "Dorry Thomas."

"Go have a seat and the doctor will see to you."

Henry waited. There were some toys there for little kids. At least you didn't have to worry about them being contaminated with infectious viruses there like at the pediatrician's office. Bobby immediately toddled over to a bright red train and played contentedly, banging it around on the floor. Henry was watching Bobby when the doctor came out and didn't see him at first.

"Henry?"

Henry looked up. He got up quickly and shook hands with the doctor.

"I think I've met you before, haven't I, Henry?"

"Yeah," Henry agreed, pursing his lips. "Last time, maybe."

"Sure. So, you're back home and settled. Your Mom is stabilized and should be able to function at home."

"Is she okay?" Henry questioned. "Was it bad this time? Clint didn't really want to talk about it."

"I think he saw the warning signs and got her in quicker than usual. She was in bad shape, but not as bad as she could be."

"Poor Ma," Henry sighed. "What is she on this time?"

The doctor carefully outlined each of the medications and how often she was to take them.

"Do any of them take away her appetite?" Henry asked. "'Cause I've been worried about her weight."

"I don't think so. The depression itself takes it away more than anything. I was going to ask you about her eating habits."

"She only eats when I check up on her, and sometimes not even then. She says she's just not hungry. I try to get her special foods I know she really likes, but money's pretty tight."

"Keep an eye on it. I want to know if she loses any more. And will you make sure she gets to her group sessions?"

"Yeah. What day?"

"Wednesday afternoon."

"Okay."

"You're a good kid. Come on, we'll go get her."

Henry picked up Bobby, who started to kick in protest at being taken from the toys. Henry got a foot in the ribs and just about dropped the baby, catching his breath sharply.

"Are you okay?" the doctor questioned, touching his arm in concern.

Henry nodded, moving stiffly. "I just hurt myself; he hit a tender spot."

Before Henry realized what he was doing, the doctor reached over and pulled Henry's t-shirt up a few inches, displaying Henry's newest bruises. Henry pulled away from him, letting the t-shirt fall back down into position.

"Just hurt myself," he murmured.

"In a fight?" the doctor tried to meet his eyes.

"Yeah. It's nothing, okay? Hardly even hurts."

The doctor was silent for a moment. "Let's get your mom," he said finally, deciding not to pursue it.

He led Henry to the small hospital room where Dorry had spent the last few weeks. She sat listlessly on the gray, flat bed, waiting. She stood up when they walked in. Henry gave her a little squeeze. Gently. She looked frail and brittle, birdlike.

"Hey, Ma. How're you feeling?"

"Oh, you know. I'm doing better now," she said without enthusiasm.

"Good."

"You got Bobby back already," she noted.

"Yeah."

"Did you tell Cheryl thank you for taking him?"

"Of course I did."

She said goodbye to the doctor. Henry took her bag from her and led the way to the car. "Do you want to drive?" he offered.

"Oh no, hon'. You drive."

"Okay."

———

Dorry started worrying the minute they got home.

"What are we going to do about your school?" she questioned, her voice rising in pitch. "You can't go back to where everybody knows what happened and where that girl's friends all go."

"Don't worry about it, Ma," he reassured her. "I'll work it out. You don't have to do anything."

"You can't do it all by yourself—" she insisted.

"Sure, I can. I'll find another school and get transferred. Don't worry about it."

She hesitated, brows drawn down, shaking her head. "Okay," she said eventually. She was silent for a few minutes, then looked at his face, brushing his hair back from his forehead. "Are you okay?" she inquired. "Are you really home for good? They aren't going to send you back there?"

"I'm home for good. That's all over," he soothed.

"I don't want to lose you like that."

He caught her hands and held them still, trying to convey a sense of calm to her. To get her to slow down and relax.

"I know, Ma. I'm okay. I'm not going anywhere. I'll take care of you."

"Oh, you don't have to take care of me," she protested. "Just… don't go away for a long time."

Henry nodded. He went to the kitchen to see if he could find something that would tempt her to eat.

32

———

Starting at a new school in the middle of the year was never much fun. And he had to bus now, which meant he either had less time with Bobby or would be late getting to school. The first day he had to meet with the principal, so he left early. He had a feeling he'd be gathering tardies after that. Bobby couldn't be left alone with Dorry for that long.

The principal didn't keep him waiting, but invited him in immediately. He was a short man, balding, red-cheeked, fussily dressed. He motioned Henry to a chair and sat down behind his desk.

"So, Henry. You'll be picking up in the middle, so you be sure to get help if you need it."

"Yeah, I will," Henry agreed.

"I notice that your marks have dropped quite a bit this year…"

"I've had some things going on."

"That's a real warning sign for us. We'll be keeping a close eye on you."

"I'm not on drugs or anything," Henry assured him.

"I hope not. We try to keep the school clean."

"You know I've had some trouble," Henry said baldly. "You don't have to pretend you haven't at least heard rumors."

The principal's face cleared.

"I'm glad you're willing to have it out in the open," he approved, relieved. "You were in jail."

"Yeah. But I was never convicted," Henry pointed out. "Never went to trial. They released me when someone else confessed."

"You had some other trouble too. Fights, trouble getting along with other students…"

"I never started anything. I never caused any trouble." Henry spread his hands. "Look, I'm a geek, right? People like to pick on geeks."

The principal sat back and considered him, rubbing his chin. "You seem like a decent kid," he observed. "But appearances can be deceiving. If you are the cause of any trouble here, you will not be welcome," he warned sternly.

Henry wondered if something about his outward appearance had changed. He'd never before had any trouble convincing schoolteachers that he really was a good kid, trying hard, and just got into trouble because of bullies or inexplicable coincidences. Was the warning just because he had been in juvie? Or did the principal think that he saw something else in Henry's face? Something that made him believe that Henry might be hiding something.

"I'm a good student," he assured. "I won't cause any trouble."

"Just as long as that's understood. Now, you have your books and schedule?"

Henry nodded. "Yes, sir."

"Okay. Let's get you a locker."

———

Henry checked the address again. He had the number right, but there was no one home. He didn't know whether he was supposed to wait around, or try again, or what. He decided to wait for a while, at least. He didn't want to get in Marty's bad books.

A girl with red hair came up the stairs and down the hall, watching Henry warily. It became apparent that she lived at the apartment that Henry was camped in front of.

"Who are you?" she questioned.

"I must have the wrong place. I was looking for the Martin place."

She was nice looking, though with a bit too much make-up, and wearing tight clothes that distracted Henry when he tried to look at her face and have a natural conversation.

"This is it," the redhead told him. "But John's in juvie; he ain't here."

"I know. I was supposed to see his mom."

"She's still working. What do you want to see her for?"

"Are you his sister?" Henry questioned. They didn't look at all alike.

"Brilliant. Yeah. What do you want?" she demanded.

Henry was unsure how to handle it. Was he supposed to talk to her? Confide in her? Or was it a secret? "I have something for her. Your mom."

"Something from John?"

"Yes. He asked me to bring it."

"Dirty money?" she guessed.

Henry shifted. "Money," he agreed.

She snorted. "Well, tell him to keep it. She doesn't need his money."

"He said to give it to his ma," Henry protested. "I gotta do what he said."

"I'm taking care of her. Stay away from here."

Henry was desperate. "Just take it. I don't care what you do with it. Throw it away. Mail it to him. I said I'd deliver it."

"Tell John that Sandy threw you out on your ear. He won't argue with that."

She succeeded in looking more stubborn than tough. Henry tried to picture Sandy and Marty growing up together as kids, but had trouble imagining it. He put his hands in his pockets, considering her.

"You're going to get me in trouble."

"You were in trouble the second you started talking to John."

Sandy was probably right. Henry was looking for a way to prolong the conversation with her, finding he was enjoying the exchange. She was nice to look at, reasonably personable. She wasn't chasing him or hanging on him, but she wasn't running away from him in fear or disgust, either. It seemed like all of the girls at school were at one end of the spectrum or the other, with no one just talking to him and treating him normally.

"How far apart are you guys in age?" he queried.

"He's seventeen, I'm fourteen."

"Me too," Henry offered with a smile.

Sandy shrugged. "You're not my type," she said flatly.

Henry was stung. He knew he was nerdy, but he was used to the attention he'd had lately. He moved away from Sandy. "At least tell your mom Marty was thinking of her," he suggested.

"Yeah, right."

Henry put Bobby down tiredly and looked around the kitchen, arching his back and rolling his shoulders. It was late, and he'd needed to get something cooking before Clint got home. He had homework to do if he was going to catch up at school too.

Unfortunately, Clint got home tired and hungry before Henry was ready for him.

"When's dinner?" he demanded grumpily.

"Soon."

"Where's your ma?"

"Still at group, I guess. I haven't seen her."

Clint looked at the dishes that were out. "What's taking so long?"

"It'll be done soon," Henry said impatiently.

"Don't take that tone with me. I expect you to take care of things around here."

"It takes longer to get home from school now," Henry said, trying to explain why he was so behind.

"Well, it ain't my fault you got in trouble at the old one."

"I didn't do anything!"

"You really think anyone believes that?" Clint questioned. "Sure, the cops let you go because they didn't have much choice. But everyone knows you were involved."

Henry was shocked. His jaw dropped and he shook his head in disbelief. "You think I did it?" he demanded incredulously.

Clint took a beer out of the fridge and pulled the tab before taking a drink. He licked his lips and wiped his mouth with the back of his hand. "Where there's smoke, there's fire. People don't just get arrested for murder when they're not guilty of something. I been there, I know."

Henry swallowed. "You've been there?" he repeated. He'd always thought Clint stupid and crude, but generally a law-abiding citizen.

Clint shrugged. "Same as you, they didn't have any proof and had to let me go."

"Who—" Henry stopped, realizing it was probably unwise to ask.

"My girlfriend's kid," Clint said evenly. At Henry's look of horror, he burst into laughter. "It's a joke, kid. I'm kidding. Hurry up and get dinner on the table."

He walked away into the living room to turn on the TV, chuckling and snorting at his own joke. Henry stared after him.

He was joking about how much of what he had said? Just that last shot about the girlfriend's son, or the whole thing?

Henry didn't know what to think.

———

Henry managed to get a hold of Marty on the weekend to discuss the errands with him.

"I took the money for your mom by," he explained. "but your sister was there."

"My sister?" Marty said blankly. "Oh—Sandy? What's she doing there?"

"Isn't she your sister?" Henry questioned, not understanding.

"Yeah. Sort of. But she doesn't live with Ma any more than I do."

"Where does she live?" Henry asked.

"With her old man, her dad. He ain't mine. She works for him, unless he's in jail or something."

"Maybe he is in jail, and that's why she was at your mom's."

"Yeah, probably. So, what'd sweet Sandy tell you?"

"She wouldn't let me give the money to your ma. Told me she was taking care of her."

"Huh. Sounds like she's still working."

"What does she do?" Henry asked curiously.

"Specs, a shorter list would be what doesn't she do," Marty laughed. "She's got her finger in just about as many pies as me. Mostly street corners and p-notes right now."

Street corners Henry could guess at. Especially with the tight, revealing clothing she had been wearing. Sandy was a prostitute.

"P-notes?" he repeated.

"Funny money. She passes counterfeit cash."

"Oh."

"You're so naive, Specs. It's funny." Marty's amusement carried down the line. Henry's face got warm, a little embarrassed.

"Yeah. What do you want me to do about it?"

"Hang onto the dough for now. Check back in a couple weeks and see if Sandy's still hanging around. As long as Ma's being looked after, it doesn't matter whose money it is."

"I can't keep that kind of money around here," Henry warned. "If my ma found it…"

"You worry too much. Your ma's not gonna find anything. You find somewhere she doesn't go and hide it there," Marty instructed, his voice steely.

"Okay," Henry agreed meekly. "I'll try to find somewhere."

———

After Henry got off the phone, he looked around for a hiding place. He discounted his room. It was too empty; anything out of place would be immediately noticed. He went down to the basement, which was dark and musty and full of old bags of clothes and broken junk. It didn't take long to find a hiding place there, and he squirreled the wad of cash away and went back upstairs.

He grinned to himself, heart thumping from the thrill of an illicit secret, and went about his chores.

33

It wasn't two weeks before he saw Sandy again They ran into each other, oddly enough, at the mall. Sandy gave Henry a start, tapping him on the shoulder as he pocketed a package of razors. He jumped and turned guiltily; sure he'd been caught lifting for a second time.

"It is you," she said. "I have a pretty good memory for people. What's your name, anyway?"

"Henry."

"Henry," she repeated, wrinkling her nose. "And this is your baby?" she indicated Bobby, sitting in the cart swinging his feet.

"Yeah. Well, not mine—my brother."

"He's a cutie. I got pregnant once," she said chattily, "but I got an abortion."

"Oh." He didn't know what to say. "Sorry."

"I got over it. Woulda been worse to have been tied down to a kid. No good for a girl. Eats up half your income in babysitting."

Henry just nodded. She was in a talkative mood; he wondered if she was high.

"So, what're you doing here?" Sandy questioned.

"Just shopping," Henry shrugged.

"Yeah, with a five-finger discount, I see."

Henry flushed, feeling hot right down to the roots of his hair. "It's a rush," he said, as if he had to explain it to her, who had a finger in so many pies.

"Try this," she put something in his hand. Henry looked down, half expecting drugs. It was money. Henry thumbed the bills apart and examined them.

"P-notes?"

"You know the lingo," she observed. "Yeah. It's fun. You get a hundred in funny money, you buy something and get good twenties back as change. You give the good twenties back to the dealer and keep what you bought."

Henry handed them back. "Cool," he approved.

"Yeah. You wanna go for ice cream or something?" she offered brightly.

"I thought I wasn't your type," Henry reminded her.

She ruffled Bobby's hair. "No, but this guy is," she leaned over and kissed Bobby square on the lips.

Henry's stomach twisted. "Don't do that," he growled, pushing in between her and Bobby.

"Don't kiss him?"

"Don't kiss him like he's grown up. He's a baby."

"What's the difference?"

"Kiss him on the cheek or forehead. Gently. Not like he's..." Henry ran out of words, not sure how to explain his reaction to her.

Sandy shrugged. "I didn't mean nothing by it," she apologized. "So, you want an ice cream or not?"

Henry looked at her for a moment. She was cute. Although she said he wasn't her type, she was the one who had offered to spend time together. She was relaxed with him, not like the other girls. More like someone who just wanted to be friends.

"Okay, sure," he agreed.

———

Dorry had been getting back later and later from group therapy lately, so Henry wasn't immediately worried that she wasn't home when he got back. But as the evening wore on, he started to get anxious. She was a 'home' person. When things got bad, she was far more likely to refuse to get out of bed than to go out and be irresponsible.

Henry called the doctor in charge of group. He had a hard time getting past the receptionist, but eventually, he convinced her he had to talk to the doctor.

"Henry Thomas," the doctor greeted cheerfully. "How's mom?"

"I don't know. What time did she leave your office?"

There was silence, and Henry knew the answer before the doctor said anything.

"Today?" the doctor asked uncertainly.

"She was supposed to be at group with you today," Henry reminded him.

"No, she transferred over to Dr. Watson's group, on Fridays. Because of her new job."

Holding the phone against his shoulder, Henry fell into a chair, his face in his hands.

How could this be happening?

"Henry, are you still there?" the doctor queried.

"Yeah," Henry said, his voice rough, barely able to get the single syllable out.

"Are you okay?"

"I don't know."

"What's going on?"

Henry swallowed hard. "She doesn't have a new job. She's been going out Wednesdays, not Friday. And… today she didn't come home."

"That's out of character for her?"

"She doesn't like to go out," Henry said. "Where's she been going if she's not going to group?" his voice cracked. He swallowed again, trying to keep the hot lump in his chest from turning into tears.

"Has her behavior changed in any other way?" the doctor's voice remained calm and even, clinical. His lack of emotion helped Henry keep from breaking down completely.

Henry tried to concentrate on the question, tried to focus on Dorry's recent behavior. How *had* she been lately?

"I don't know. I didn't notice anything, except her staying later at group the last little while."

"Well, maybe she'll still show up."

"Maybe," Henry agreed, not hopeful.

"Take care, Henry."

Henry said goodbye and hung up the phone.

———

That night, Bobby was fussy, hot and flushed with fever. Henry cuddled with him, trying to quiet him back to sleep. Bobby whined and held Henry around the neck, pressing his burning face against Henry's chest.

"Shut up!" Clint shouted from the other room.

Henry held Bobby close. "Please, shh, it's okay," Henry whispered anxiously. "Shh… come on, Bobby. Don't keep Clint up."

He could hear Clint's bedsprings squeak and got up nervously. He went into the kitchen to see if a drink would calm Bobby down.

Bobby started to cry in earnest when Henry turned the light on. Henry heard Clint's feet hit the floor with a bang and turned in panic.

That was followed by a blank. Henry didn't remember the confrontation with Clint. He didn't remember leaving the house or where he went or what he thought after that. He remembered Clint getting out of bed and the next thing Henry was aware of was that he was pounding on the door of the emergency shelter.

"Get out of here or we'll call the police," someone shouted from inside.

"You gotta let me in," Henry shouted back. "Come on, please."

"You wanna talk to the cops?"

"I need to get in," Henry pleaded.

There was no further response from the building. Henry banged on the door until his fists were bruised and sore. He sat down on the curb in front of the shelter, sobbing. He didn't look up when a car pulled up and someone walked up behind him.

"Move on, kid. Or we're going to have to take you in," a man's voice warned.

"I can't go," Henry protested, his voice still teary.

"You've got a girlfriend in there," the cop suggested. "And you don't think you can wait to work things out. We see it here every day. But you can wait until she decides to come to you."

Henry shook his head. They had it all wrong.

"I need somewhere to stay. I need someone to help with my baby," he said.

The cop came closer, coming around in front of Henry. For the first time, the cop saw that the bundle Henry held was not a knapsack or bedroll, but a baby wrapped up in Henry's coat. He shone his flashlight in Henry's face. He sat down on the curb next to Henry. He moved the coat aside to examine Bobby's face.

"Is he okay?"

"He's sick. We can't sleep outside."

"What happened?"

Henry shook his head. "I don't know. We had to go." Everything was muddled; he couldn't even get the words out properly. "Why won't they let me in?"

"You rest here a minute. I'll see what I can work out."

The cop was gone for a while, talking on the doorstep of the shelter while Henry hunched dejectedly on the curb. The man returned and patted him on the back.

"Come on, buddy."

"What?"

"Come on," the cop repeated, and gave Henry a hand up. He led Henry to the open door. A man in wrinkled gray sweats met him.

"Come on in, son. Sorry for the misunderstanding."

Henry was tired, his mind foggy. He just wanted to go to bed and let consciousness seep away. Like at the prison, he could feel his brain grinding to a halt, refusing to allow him to function any longer. He looked around inside for somewhere to put Bobby down. The man took Bobby gently.

"I'll just put him in a crib while we take care of you."

"He's sick," Henry murmured. "Has a fever."

The man felt Bobby's head. "A bit of one. Not bad. Best to just let him sleep. We'll have him looked at in the morning."

He took Bobby out of the room and returned a few minutes later.

"There, he'll be fine for now," he assured Henry. "Let's take care of you."

Henry sat down in the chair the man motioned to.

"My name is Jonathan. What's yours?"

Henry had no energy at all for invention. He sat hunched in the chair. "Henry."

"What happened tonight, Henry?" Jonathan questioned.

"I don't know."

Jonathan brought out a white metal first aid kit with a red cross on it. Henry watched listlessly as he took out antiseptic wipes and gauze.

"Take off your glasses," Jonathan said. Henry obeyed without understanding why. Jonathan dabbed at Henry's cheek with a piece of gauze and Henry was surprised to see it come away red with blood. He touched his face with exploratory fingers. It was swollen, seeping blood, but Henry had no pain sensation. Jonathan moved Henry's hand away in order to continue his work. Henry's lids grew heavy, and he started to nod. He was barely conscious of being taken to bed and lying down.

34

So what happened last night, Henry?" Jonathan questioned the next day. "Tell me a little bit about your situation."

Henry noticed a blood speck on his glasses and cleaned them carefully. He put them back on his face gingerly. The numbness of the previous night was gone and the bruises did hurt.

"I don't know," Henry said. "My mom's disappeared. Bobby was sick and crying."

"It wasn't Bobby who hit you," Jonathan observed with a slight smile.

"You can't tell anyone," Henry pleaded.

"I don't even know your last name," Jonathan reminded him. "I can't report anything. But I want to help. Can't you tell me?"

"Clay," Henry said, deciding at the last minute that perhaps using their proper names was risky. "My mom's... boyfriend. He just gets mean sometimes."

"Where's your dad?" Jonathan questioned. "Could you stay with him?"

"Don't have one."

"So you're trying to take care of Bobby on your own? How can you manage that with school?"

"Oh, I get help," Henry assured Jonathan, to keep him from getting too concerned or involved. "It isn't that bad."

"Do you guys live with Clay? Something should be done about that."

"N-no." Henry thought fast. "I'm staying with a buddy, since mom moved out of Clay's place. I just… went back for something for Bobby's fever. A lot of our stuff is still there."

"Well, it's good that you're not living there. You're safe at this friend's house? Is it a long-term arrangement?"

"Yeah. You know, I help out with chores and take care of Bobby, try to keep it from being too much extra work for his folks. They're okay with it 'til I'm old enough to take Bobby on my own."

Wouldn't it be nice if he really did have a friend like that? It sounded like a really nice arrangement.

"What about college?" Jonathan questioned.

"It's four years 'til I graduate, then he'll be in kindergarten," Henry paused. "That's a long way away."

"Yes, it is. But you need to be thinking ahead when you're making major decisions."

Just thinking a day ahead made Henry's stomach tight with anxiety. "I should be going," he suggested. "I gotta take Bobby to the doctor and take care of things."

"Okay. You come back if you get in a jam. Knock and tell us who it is. We know you now, we'll take you in. I'm sorry about the confusion last night. We get a lot of irate boyfriends and have the police on speed-dial."

"Yeah, okay," Henry agreed. "I didn't mean to worry anyone. I was just… sorta panicked."

"We're here if you need us again."

Henry nodded gratefully. "Yeah, thanks."

———

Henry walked into the house.

He was anxious, feeling like someone was watching him. Something was out of place, not quite right. He looked around carefully. Had someone been in the house? Was someone there now?

The shoes looked wrong. Like someone had cleaned or straightened them. He looked around the kitchen, but everything seemed normal there. He looked in the master bedroom and his heart thudded heavily. It was empty. Henry had cleaned up Dorry's things earlier in the week. Now Clint's stuff was gone. The room was picked clean.

Henry breathed a sigh of relief. Clint had made it clear from the start that he was there for Dorry. If she was out for long, he would leave. If she was at the clinic, he often took off for days or weeks. Now, when it became apparent that she was gone, maybe for good, he had cleared out.

Henry and Bobby were on their own.

———

It was hard.

Henry was missing a lot of school, but studying and doing his homework to keep up. It was hard leaving Bobby alone during the day. Henry got to school late, went home at lunch, and sometimes skipped his last class. He put videos on the TV in Bobby's room and left him with extra bottles and snacks. The room was babyproofed, but he still worried Bobby would learn how to open the door and get into trouble.

Trouble came in another form, however. A social worker, called by someone who had noticed the lack of parents recently. Henry was making sandwiches in the kitchen when she arrived. He answered the doorbell, and his stomach tightened. The woman was obviously a social worker. He knew that by the drab skirt and blazer before he even saw the ID tag.

"Yeah?" he

"Are your parents home, son?" she asked pleasantly, trying to look around him.

Henry swallowed. "They're out."

"Mind if I come in?"

"I'm not supposed to let people in when I'm alone," Henry blocked her, not letting her get past him.

She indicated the Family Services badge that she wore around her neck. "I'm with Protective Services. I'd like to have a look around."

Henry was torn. "I guess," he conceded finally.

She came in and looked around. "So, where's your Mom at?"

"She goes for therapy."

"I see," she made a note on her clipboard. "Is she capable of caring for you and your brother?"

"Usually," Henry said, trying to stick close to the truth. "I help out as much as I can with Bobby."

She observed Bobby toddling around for a moment, then continued on her tour. "So, someone is here during the day?" she checked.

"Yeah."

"Bobby's never left alone?"

"No."

Henry was sweating. His heart was racing and he was nervous about everything that she looked at. He waited tensely for her to go.

"Do you need any help?"

"No, we're doing okay," Henry assured her. "If you have a card, then I can call if I do need something."

"Of course," she pulled one out and handed it to him.

"Thanks. I'll call you."

She looked in each of the bedrooms. "I think you're the only one living here," she suggested quietly.

"No," Henry said flatly.

"I'll be back to check up in a few days," she promised. Or

threatened. It was friendly and soft, but it was really more of a threat than a promise.

"Okay," Henry said, trying to force a smile. "Maybe Ma will be here next time."

She left after a bit more snooping around. Henry watched her retreat down the sidewalk and get into her car. He pulled his sweaty shirt away from his body and ran nervous fingers through his hair. He sat down at the kitchen table and tried to work out what he was going to do.

35

It won't be for long," Henry coaxed Sandy. "I just need a place to stay for a few days to figure out what to do next."

"What's the problem?" Sandy countered, shaking her head. "You just let them take Bobby and put him in foster care. Then you're free to do what you like."

"I'm the only family he's got now. We have to stick together," Henry explained.

"What is this, a Hallmark movie? This is real life. Families don't stay together anymore."

"Well, I want me and Bobby to stay together "

"Good luck," she said, rolling her eyes.

"So, can I stay at your place for a day or two? Just until I find somewhere else?" Henry asked again.

"Don't you have any friends?" Sandy demanded.

"Not really," Henry admitted. There was no one at the new school. No one that he could ask. "But me and Marty were pretty tight in juvie…"

"So? I don't owe you anything."

"I know, I just thought…"

He had hoped to use the family connection to convince her, but he could see that wasn't going to work.

"John and I don't see eye to eye," Sandy pointed out. "Don't expect anything from me, just 'cause you and him were friendly."

"What about for Bobby?" Henry challenged grumpily. "You said you like him, even if you don't like me."

"Yeah, he's cute. But I also told you I don't want a kid," she reminded him.

Henry flopped down on a park bench and watched Bobby play in the sand. "What am I gonna do?" he said in frustration, his voice cracking a little.

Sandy shrugged unsympathetically. "You're fourteen, Thomas; you're old enough to take care of yourself. Plenty of kids on the street our age and younger. There's lots of ways to make some money, keep yourself alive."

"I know," Henry agreed, "but I don't want to be involved in anything... wrong."

Sandy looked at him in disbelief, and he was afraid he had hurt her feelings. It wasn't like she earned her living honestly.

"Who do you think you are?" Sandy demanded incredulously. "You've been in juvie, you're running errands for John's enterprises, you're shoplifting, and you're kidnapping Bobby. You don't want to do anything 'wrong'? Who do you think you're kidding?"

"Bobby's mine. I'm not kidnapping him," Henry protested, fastening on that.

She shook her head impatiently. "I ain't gonna argue law with you. But he isn't your son, unless you're lying to me, and courts don't give custody to kids like you unless they are the real parents."

"Yeah," Henry said thoughtfully.

Sandy's eyes narrowed. "What are you cooking up now?"

Henry looked at her, frowning. His thoughts were racing ahead. "You have contacts, right?" he asked.

"What kind of contacts?" Sandy's brows drew down. She swept her long red hair over her shoulders.

"Someone who could give me documents saying that Bobby's my son."

"Why would you wanna go and do something like that?" Sandy questioned, obviously thinking him crazy. "Besides, Family Services already knows he's your brother."

"Not if I change my name. They won't know the difference."

"You don't want to do that, Thomas," she warned. "Trust me; you don't want to do that at all."

———

Henry knocked on the door. It wasn't Jonathon that opened it this time. The tall, spidery man looked Henry and Bobby over.

"Yes?" he said cautiously.

"I got kicked out. I need somewhere to stay—just tonight."

The man stepped back to allow Henry in, his eyes still wary. "Are you the kid who was here the other night?"

Henry nodded. "Yeah—I talked to Jonathan."

The man seemed to relax a little at the mention of his colleague by name. He extended his hand. "I'm Ron."

"Henry."

"You got kicked out?" Ron asked, leading him into the shelter.

"Yeah."

"By your folks?"

"No, I was staying with a friend."

"Where are your folks?"

Henry shrugged and fussed with Bobby's jacket and hat. "Gone," he said flatly.

"And this little guy is your brother?"

Henry was pretty sure he had referred to Bobby as 'his' baby to Jonathan, as he usually did, and had never clarified that they were brothers.

"No, he's my kid," he said evenly. The intentional lie would get easier, but he was sweating, his mouth suddenly dry. Ron didn't appear to detect the lie. When he turned his back for a moment, Henry wiped the sweat from his forehead.

"You're pretty young to be a father."

If he was fourteen, then Bobby was conceived when he was twelve. Not impossible, but a little hard to believe. Henry had already thought about that. His new ID put him at sixteen, a father at fourteen or fifteen. More believable. He tried to put on a manly swagger for Ron.

"Yeah, a little," he agreed boldly.

"Where's the baby's mom?"

"I don't know where she is right now. I've had Bobby since he was tiny. Haven't seen her in a long time."

"Well, why don't you get him settled in, and then we can discuss options."

Henry nodded. "Do you think you can help me figure something out?"

Ron smiled reassuringly. "You bet. We'll work something out."

"What about foster care for a few years?" Ron suggested as they discussed options later. "The two of you together in a foster home until you're old enough to take care of yourselves on your own."

"I'm not doin' that. I want to work it so I can keep taking care of him now."

"It's not going to be easy," Ron warned.

"It's never been easy."

"Are you going to work or go to school?"

"I gotta finish school."

"Good. You'll need to apply for welfare and housing. Food stamps. Subsidized daycare. There are a lot of ways to get help."

"Some of the schools have programs for teen parents," Henry suggested.

"Well, moms. I never heard of a dad getting into the program."

"But I'm the caregiver."

"Yes, you are. I'll look into it, but don't get your hopes up. And you're going to need to stay here for more than a day. Until you get housing of your own. It might be a while, and you don't want to be bouncing back and forth between homes in that time. Children need consistency and order. It's not good to be taking Bobby all kinds of places."

"Okay," Henry agreed.

"We'll get started tomorrow. You get a good sleep tonight."

36

Henry checked his camera settings to make sure he was ready to go. He loved the art class in the single parents' program. He got to choose what medium to use—pencils, paint, photography, clay, whatever. And he could use whatever style, method, or effects he wanted to use. The focus was on finding a way to express himself through whatever medium worked the best for him. Henry had felt immediately at home with the camera. He loved to develop his own film, and the teacher liked his work. They had done some still life, had gone to the zoo, had looked at old, abandoned farm buildings, and even brought a couple of the babies into the class as models. Today they were going to have a woman come model for them, as they studied the human figure as a subject. Everyone was ready and eager to get going.

A woman came into the class in a robe and looked around, smiling. Her eyes stopped on Henry, and she turned and spoke to the teacher. Henry couldn't hear her but knew what she was saying. Mrs. Clark hadn't told her there was a boy in the single parents' program. They spoke in lowered voices for a few minutes.

"She won't pose for you," Sherri commented to Henry, a little bit accusing.

"It's not my fault."

"Tell Mrs. Clark you'll sit this one out," she suggested.

"No, I don't want to miss it!"

"You're going to make all of us miss it."

Mrs. Clark motioned for Henry to join her. He followed her and the model out into the hallway.

"Henry, Adrienne is nervous about posing with you there."

Henry shrugged. "Why? It's for an art subject, I'm not going to whistle or catcall."

"Would you like to show her some of the stuff in your portfolio? I've been trying to explain you're not the average sixteen-year-old boy…"

"Sure," Henry agreed. "Most of it's in the darkroom."

He led the way and pulled down a few of his recent pictures from the drying line. He handed them to Adrienne.

"These are Bobby, my baby," he said, and rifled through his photo box. "And some of the animals and still lifes we've done."

"These are very good," Adrienne admitted. She looked over some of the other pictures of Bobby that were hung up. "Bobby is adorable."

"I think so. He's pretty photogenic."

"Do you have any of his mom?" she suggested.

"No. She's not around."

"Henry is raising Bobby alone," Mrs. Clark said.

"Oh, of course."

"I made a mistake," Henry admitted, "but I take responsibility and I'm working hard to make sure that it doesn't ruin the rest of my life—or Bobby's."

She studied him frankly. "You are very mature for sixteen," she said eventually.

She didn't know the half of it. He looked down and shrugged modestly.

"I'll do it," Adrienne agreed. "I'll model for you. You are an artist."

They went back to the classroom. Without another word, Adrienne went to the center of the room and shed her robe. Henry picked up his camera and started snapping pictures.

———

Bobby had finally gone down to sleep. Henry got out his pictures to look at. The pictures of Adrienne had turned out really well. Her smooth, flawless skin and dark features contrasted with the stark white backdrop. He loved her figure, so much fuller and more mature than the girls Henry's age.

He wanted to see her again.

To take more pictures.

He had asked Mrs. Clark for Adrienne's full name so he could label the photos correctly, and she had given it to him. He looked in the phone book, and there were several addresses to check out. He would start with the closest one.

Henry put his camera with a telephoto lens in his bag and went out.

He had to wait a while at the first address. No one was home when he got there. But Henry waited and watched the windows, and eventually, she got home. He got a couple shots of her closing the drapes, and that was all. But he went home satisfied.

Knowing where she lived, he could follow her and build a collection of candid shots.

———

Henry was surprised how much food the subsidies got him.

He was used to trying to feed a family on whatever disability money his mom didn't spend first, and some weeks that meant just

Kraft dinner and Kool-Aid. With the welfare programs he qualified for, he had plenty for balanced meals for himself and Bobby. They even gave him money to spend on other things after the rent was paid. Mostly, he bought photography equipment to set up a darkroom of his own so he didn't have to develop all of his pictures at the school where others might see them. If he needed other, more expensive materials, he borrowed them from the school darkroom.

Along with the candid shots of Adrienne, he had some of her neighbors, who he could sometimes see through their windows when she was not visible. He was trying to expand his interests and subjects, though he found himself increasingly preoccupied with getting more pictures of Adrienne.

She had a quality that no one else he photographed even approached.

"So, what else are you up to lately?" Marty questioned lazily. Henry was eager to get off the phone, but Marty wasn't letting him go. Henry didn't like to be mixed up with Marty, but was afraid that Marty would implicate him if he broke off communications.

"Nothing," Henry said. "Just school."

"What're you doing at school?" Marty pressed.

"I dunno. Just stuff. Photography."

"For real? You're taking pictures for school?" Marty questioned, sounding interested.

"Yeah." Henry wasn't sure why Marty sounded so excited about it.

"Develop your own film?"

"Sure."

"I can hook you up with some other guys into that," Marty suggested.

Henry hesitated. "Really?"

"Sure. I know a couple guys really into pictures. I'll put them in touch with you."

"Okay," Henry agreed, nodding even though Marty couldn't see him.

Henry thought it might be interesting to get together with a couple of hobbyists who had a bit more experience than him. He was learning a lot at school, but he could learn so much more from others who were out there in the field and had spent years developing their skills.

———

The apartment that welfare had put Henry in was just a couple of blocks away from Sandy's pad, and he occasionally ran into her at the grocery store or other places in the neighborhood. He never mentioned to Marty that he was still in contact with her.

Bobby climbed up the steps on the small slide. While Henry watched Bobby, he saw Sandy across the park, apparently closing some sort of deal with an unsavory-looking man. She glanced around quickly. Henry saw her stop, looking in his direction. After she and the gentleman separated, she walked over to where Henry was standing.

"I don't like people stickin' their noses in my business."

"I'm just watching Bobby. I noticed you were there. That isn't snooping."

"How come I see you everywhere I go?" she accused.

Henry shrugged. "I just see you around the neighborhood."

"First I hear you're into taking pictures, then I see you hanging around all the time."

"You heard about me taking pictures?" Henry repeated.

"Yeah, some of John's boys wanted to know how to contact you. People around here don't like cameras, Thomas, you better watch your step," she warned.

"Thomson," Henry corrected. "I'm not hurting anyone taking pictures."

"Sure."

"I don't even have a camera with me right now. So, what are you worried about?"

"I don't know; you could have a spy camera, one of those little things. I don't like people taking pictures of me."

Henry wouldn't have pegged her as the type to be camera shy. He shrugged and watched Bobby play.

<h1 style="text-align:center">37</h1>

It was dark when there was a knock on Henry's door. He was getting ready to go out, and it startled him. No one should be coming to his apartment so late. Probably just someone knocking on the wrong door. Ignore it, and they would go away. He waited.

A louder knock, more insistent this time. Henry bit his lip.

"Go away," he muttered and waited some more.

The next minute, the door was kicked in. Henry stood there for an instant, stunned, before looking for cover. His feet froze to the floor. He dragged himself behind the couch in slow motion. It was stupid to be hiding behind the couch with the two of them standing there watching him. But he did it anyway.

"That our bird?" one of the boys questioned.

The other boy walked around the couch and looked at him. "Yeah," he chuckled, "that's our bird."

"Stand him up."

Henry stood up when the boy put his hand under his arm. He swallowed, trying to find his voice. "What are you doing here?" he squeaked.

The other boy shut the door quietly.

"We're just here for a little visit, Henry," he said gravely, "or should I call you Specs?"

"Specs?" Henry repeated hoarsely.

They were Marty's boys.

"Yeah. I'm Richards. This is Hans."

Richards and Hans looked around the apartment, and without asking leave, started looking through drawers and checking out the rest of the suite. Henry watched, unable to comprehend what was going on.

"Yeah, in here, Richie," Hans called from the bathroom. Richards joined him. Henry followed them and watched helplessly as they pulled down his latest pictures from the string.

"Mmm," Richards murmured. "Not bad, Specs. So what direction are you going with these lovely candids? Porn? Blackmail? Both?"

"No," Henry protested, suddenly understanding Marty's and Sandy's strange behavior on finding out he was a photographer. "No, they're just—" how could he explain them? He became painfully aware of his dark clothing and the camera around his neck. "They're personal," he finished lamely.

"They're all the same girl," Richards observed thoughtfully. He studied each. "You stalking her, or what?"

"Of course not," Henry said, shocked.

Richards put the pictures down on the counter abruptly. "We got a job for you," he said.

"I don't want a job."

"Did I ask if you wanted a job? We got a job for you."

"What?"

"Say you'll take it."

"What is it?" Henry insisted.

"Say you'll take it," Richard repeated firmly.

"No. Tell me what it is."

Richard put his arm around Henry's shoulders and squeezed

them in a friendly gesture. "You're gonna take it, Specs. Marty says you're taking it and now Richie says you're taking it. So, you're taking it."

Henry stood there and said nothing, just looking at him.

"So, you're doing it," Richards prompted.

Henry shrugged morosely.

"We just want you to take a few pics," Richards said, framing his face with his hands and smiling. "That's all."

Henry doubted that was all.

———

Henry dropped Bobby at the school daycare and went to his first couple of classes. Then he approached one of his teachers.

"I'm going to go home for a bit…" he started out.

"Are you all right?"

"I'm not feeling too well," Henry explained.

"You don't look so hot," she said sympathetically.

Henry was sweating and felt flushed. He probably looked like he had the flu. But he didn't.

"Why don't you leave Bobby here and get some sleep? Come back for him at the end of the day," she suggested.

"Do you think it would be okay?"

"Of course."

"That would really help."

"Go ahead," the teacher urged.

"Okay. I'll do it."

But Henry didn't go home. He went nervously to the apartment at the address Richie had given him. He rang the bell, his heart pounding, and pasted on a smile. A man with a couple day's growth of beard answered the door.

"I'm the photographer," Henry explained.

The man motioned for him to enter, not saying a word. He went into the back room. "Katie, he's here."

Henry stood awkwardly in the front room until the man turned to him.

"In here," he said impatiently.

Henry followed him. Katie was a young girl, twelve or thirteen. She was lounging on the bed in a robe. Henry stood there staring at her.

"Take it off," the man told Katie. Who was he, her father or boyfriend?

Katie obeyed, sliding the robe off. Henry raised his camera, blanking his mind, trying to concentrate on technical issues—camera angles and body form. The man owed money to Marty's boys, and some of the debt would be written off for pictures. It was a business deal; that was all—just business. One photo session and it would all be over. Henry would be out of the picture.

———

Richards showed up at Henry's apartment before the pictures were done drying. Henry let him in with a shrug of irritation. Richie went into the darkroom and examined the hanging pictures.

"Aw, Specs," he groaned. "What is this garbage? You trying to be artsy, or what?"

"What's wrong with it?" Henry questioned.

"Sheesh, just look at it! We don't want sensitive treatment and cute positioning. We want skin. Explicit. Provocative. Nothing left to the imagination. This… I dunno, you can try to pass it off as kiddie stuff, but she's pretty old for that bunch."

Henry shrugged. "You said just snap some pictures."

"You knew what we wanted."

"I guess I'm not your guy."

"Oh, that's it, is it? You figure you botch this job we won't give you another? Nice try. You'll do it 'til you get it right."

Henry shook his head. "I can't do this stuff."

"Where's your negatives?"

Henry pointed. Richards picked them up. He pulled out a card and wrote on the back of it—another address.

"This one tomorrow," he said.

"No."

"You do this one right; you'll get paid for both jobs."

"Keep your money," Henry snapped.

Richards put the card into Henry's shirt pocket.

"You do it. Or you'll be sorry."

Richards left, slamming the door. Henry heard Bobby stir and cry. He waited to see if Bobby was going to wake up all the way or not. Bobby settled again and went back to sleep.

———

Henry decompressed by going out to take pictures. Real art, not pornography. He followed Adrienne from her apartment to the bus. He couldn't follow her farther than that. If he got on the bus, she would see him, maybe recognize him from her session at the school. Henry wasn't exactly unobtrusive with a camera hanging from his neck.

He snapped a couple of pictures of her as the bus pulled away. There was a big, firm hand on his shoulder, startling him. Henry tensed, trying to pull away.

"What are you up to, son?" a gruff voice demanded.

Henry turned. A cop. Big, heavyset, in uniform. Henry swallowed and broke out into a sweat. His heart raced and he looked for some escape route. He swallowed again. There was no need to run away. He wasn't doing anything against the law.

"Just taking some pictures for an assignment at school," he explained.

"Yeah, sure," the cop countered sarcastically, "dressed like a cat burglar."

"I like black."

"You're out late. If you're going to take pictures, take them during the day. Don't go lurking around in the dark."

"Okay," Henry said, shrugging.

The cop studied him with a frown. "Let me see the camera," he said, holding out his hand.

Henry hesitated, staring into the cop's eyes. The man acted pleasant enough, but his eyes were unwavering, steel. Henry reluctantly handed the camera over.

"It's my camera," he said tentatively. "It's not stolen."

The cop took it and turned it over. Before Henry realized what he was going to do, the cop popped open the back and ripped out the film. Henry gasped in shock.

"That's mine! You can't do that!" he protested, his voice going up in a squeak.

The cop dropped the film on the ground and pushed the camera into Henry's hands.

"Stay out of my neighborhood with that. Or next time, it will be the camera you lose."

Pictures of Adrienne.

The cop had destroyed pictures of Adrienne.

Henry bit his lip, holding back tears. No cop had any right to destroy his pictures. His property. His Adrienne.

It felt as if the cop was trying to destroy Adrienne, to destroy what Henry had with her.

"You had no right to do that," Henry said, voice quavering.

"This is my beat," the cop said evenly. "I don't put up with young punks causing trouble on my beat."

"I'm not causing any trouble," Henry's voice cracked. "You can't do that!"

"And who are you going to complain to? Who are you going to tell that you were out sneaking around in the dark snapping pictures?"

Of course, there was no one he could go to. And the pictures of Adrienne were lost forever.

"Don't come back here again," the cop warned when Henry couldn't answer.

Henry looked down the street toward Adrienne's apartment building. He couldn't stay away.

The cop caught the look. "I'll be watching for you," he warned. "You stay away."

38

Henry looked at the article in the paper. He couldn't believe the picture of Adrienne that they had used. What did they do, take the picture off of her driver's license? It was awful. She was a beautiful model. Even if she was just an amateur, there must have been hundreds of flattering photos of her out there. Photos that would reproduce well in the paper.

Henry approached his teacher with the newspaper in hand. "Mrs. Clark? Isn't this the lady that modeled for us that day?"

Mrs. Clark turned to him and looked down at the paper. Her eyes were swollen and red-rimmed. She sniffled and shook her head, pressing her fingers to her temples.

"Yes," she agreed. "It's just so horrible. I can't understand how something like this could happen. Who would do something so awful?"

"Yeah," Henry agreed. He hesitated to go on. "The pictures that they're using are terrible," he pointed out. "Do you think… I have some good ones. Black and whites. They'd be great for the papers."

Mrs. Clark considered it, looking down at the newspaper in Henry's hand. "You did some headshots?" she questioned.

"Yeah."

"Well, I don't know. I guess it's a chance for you to get some exposure."

He could tell she didn't like the idea of him capitalizing on her friend's murder. It was just so gruesome.

"Maybe if there's better pictures in the paper, there's a better chance of them catching the killer," he suggested. "Somebody might recognize her face. They won't from this one."

"Yes," her frown lightened a little, "if they could find this guy… it's the least that we could do for her."

———

Richards came by to pick up the pictures. Henry had them ready in an envelope, hoping to get rid of Richie at the door. But the other boy pushed his way in anyway. He sprawled on the couch, opening the envelope and looking through the prints. He said nothing, chewing and cracking his gum, looking through them slowly, one at a time. He eventually nodded and slid them back into the envelope.

"Much better, you've got the hang of it now," he approved.

The pictures were disgusting. Henry hated them. He wanted them out of his apartment. Richards pulled out a wad of cash and threw it on the table, perhaps sensing Henry wouldn't want to take it directly from him. Henry looked at the carelessly discarded bundle of hundreds, and alarm bells went off in his head.

"If those are p-notes, try again," he told Richards sharply.

Richie's jaw dropped in astonishment. He stared at Henry for a moment and started laughing.

"You're learning pretty quick, aren't you?" he questioned, stifling his giggles and picking up the hundreds. He took out another bundle and carefully counted off twenties. He left them loose on the table. "There you go, Specs. Genuine T-bills."

T for treasury, meaning real currency. Henry waited for Richie to leave. Looking at the money on the table, he realized he would be able to afford some good photography equipment. Richards started to get up, then saw the newspaper on the table, Adrienne's picture front and center.

"Shame, she was actually pretty good-looking, huh?" Richards commented, studying Adrienne's picture. "Shame when a cute chickie like that gets offed for no reason."

Henry started to panic. His heart raced and he could barely breathe. He tried to look casual while sweat trickled down his back. Richards looked at the picture too long. Too intently. Henry moved into the kitchenette behind Richards.

"You got what you wanted," Henry said brusquely. "Don't you have someone else to harass? "No." Richards slowly raised his eyes from the paper. "This is one of yours, ain't it, Specs?" Richie started to turn around to look at Henry, his eyes glinting. "Ain't this your flame?"

He turned the rest of the way around, grinning like a wolf. Henry was right behind him with the kitchen knife he had just dried off and Richards practically walked into the blade.

Henry looked at the clock and noted the time. He was going to have to move fast. Bobby would be waking up from his nap. And though Richards had not brought any muscle with him since that first day, there might be someone close by, waiting for him to return.

Henry kicked Richie from the carpet to the floor so he wouldn't bleed into the rug. Richards made a strangled gurgling sound and moved jerkily. Henry went to the closet and took out his raincoat. He threaded Richards's arms through it and did up the buttons in the front. It was awkward, but the really difficult task was still coming.

"Come on, man, let's get you some help," he encouraged.

A gleam of hope came into Richards' dying eyes, and he managed to raise some strength to help Henry get him back on his feet. He was weak and heavy.

"Come on, we'll get you to a doctor."

With great effort, Henry was able to half-drag, half-carry

Richards down the outside hall and to the stairs. The stairs took even greater, herculean effort. He kept murmuring to Richards, encouraging him, trying to keep him moving his feet and taking a little of his weight. He prayed that they wouldn't run into anyone in the stairwell. But people were pretty lazy; they didn't usually use the stairs if the elevator was working.

They finally reached the basement and Henry dropped Richards to the floor.

"Good job," he approved.

———

Henry mopped the floor and put the bloody cloths and raincoat in the garbage. He looked at the calendar. It would not be garbage day until Thursday. He would have to wait to take it out. It couldn't sit out there in the bin where it might attract attention or be discovered by the police.

Bobby woke up and Henry gave him a snack, looking around the apartment for anything out of place. Everything was quiet. The money was still on the table. Henry picked it up and put it in his room in his cash box. He went back to the living room. There was a loud knock on the door. Henry took his time answering it. It was Hans.

"I thought Richie was coming," Henry challenged.

Hans looked confused. "He didn't come?" he asked, glancing around.

"He said he'd be here an hour ago," Henry said impatiently. He handed the envelope of photos to Hans. "I've been waiting."

Hans took the package uncertainly, as if he didn't know what to do with it.

"You have the money?" Henry questioned. "I'm supposed to be paid for both jobs."

Hans hesitated and reached into his pocket. He pulled out a money clip and thumbed some bills off—more hundred-dollar p-notes. Henry took them without comment. He had all of

Richards's p-notes, T-bills, and now p-notes from Hans too. Not a bad profit for a couple of photoshoots.

"Richie never came?" Hans asked with a frown.

"No."

"He came into the building. I saw that."

"He never came up here. I was here the whole time, waiting. Did he have someone else to see?"

"Yeah, but she—" Hans stopped himself and clamped his mouth shut. He didn't know what to do. He had obviously not been chosen for his brains. He looked around the apartment, lost.

"If he shows up… tell him to call me," Henry said.

"Sure," Hans said faintly.

Hans left, looking as forlorn as a lost child. Henry waited for the door to close, then grinned to himself. He was just getting warmed up.

———

Henry didn't know how often anyone went into the basement, so he didn't know how long it would be before the body was discovered and the police showed up. He thought it might even be a few days, but by nightfall, there were sirens and flashing lights on the street in front of the building. They knocked on his door while he was putting Bobby to bed. Henry answered the door, leaving the chain on.

"Yeah?"

"Police. We'd like to ask you a few questions."

"Umm, okay." He closed the door to take the chain off, then opened the door for them. "I have to check on the baby. Have a seat for a second."

They sat down by the table and waited. Henry checked in on Bobby, patting him on the back and turning on his music player. Bobby's eyes were already closing. Henry watched him for a few minutes, then went back out to talk to the cops.

They stood up for introductions when he returned.

"Officers Dawson and Cruz," Dawson told him, shaking hands.

"Henry Thompson."

"Are your folks in?" Dawson asked.

"I live by myself. Just me and my son."

"Oh," they readjusted their thinking. "Have you been in all day?"

"Yeah, most of the day," Henry agreed.

"Have you had any visitors?"

"Yeah." They waited for more, and Henry shrugged. "What's going on?"

"We are investigating a murder in the building."

"Really? Whoa. I didn't hear anything. Was it on this floor?"

"We don't have a lot of information yet. We're just trying to find out who was around when and if anyone heard or saw anything suspicious," Dawson explained.

Henry nodded.

"You see anyone in the hallway? Neighbors, people from the neighborhood, anyone you didn't know?"

"I don't know. I went down to get the mail..." Henry thought back, but couldn't remember seeing anyone. "Maybe saw someone from the building, but nothing out of place."

"Is that the only time you went out?"

"Umm, I took the garbage out when Bobby was sleeping this afternoon. I didn't see anyone then, I don't think. Things are pretty quiet in the afternoon."

"And you had company."

"Just a casual friend. Guy who lives in the neighborhood. Came by to see if I wanted some movie tickets for the new Disney movie," Henry pointed to them on the table. "I just see him in the building sometimes; he knows I have a kid, so..."

"What's his name?" Dawson questioned.

"Mmm, Hans or something. A German name."

"That's not a terribly common name," Dawson said thoughtfully.

"Is he in one of the gangs?" Cruz suggested.

They knew who Hans was. Henry hadn't expected them to recognize him just by his name. Henry displayed shock, giving them a wide-eyed innocent stare.

"In a gang? Gee, not that I know of. But I don't really know anything about him. I guess he could be. I don't know how I would find out."

"Unless you were in one too."

Henry laughed. "Me? Do I look like a gang banger to you? I'm a student and a single parent. I don't have time for extra-curricular activities."

"You obviously had some time for extra-curricular activities before your son was born," Dawson took over the questioning.

"Yeah, girls, not gangs. I made a mistake once and I'm paying for that for the next seventeen years."

"Yeah. So, besides this Hans, no one else came by?"

"No, not that I remember."

"Didn't run any errands? Buy milk or go to the park?"

"No. Not today. I had stuff to do around here."

"If you think of something, even if it's something small, will you give us a call?" Dawson produced a business card.

"Yeah, sure," Henry agreed.

They left, apparently suspecting nothing.

39

H enry dialed the phone. It rang a few times, then someone picked it up.

"Yeah?" the male voice questioned sharply.

"Who's this?" Henry questioned.

"Marco. Who do you want?"

"Is Richie there?" Henry tried.

"No. Who's this?"

"What about Hans?" Henry suggested.

"Yeah, he's here. Who is it?"

"Uh, Henry. Specs."

"Hang on."

There was silence for a few minutes while he was on hold, and then Hans answered. "Specs?" he queried. "Richie show up there?" he asked hopefully.

"No. I was just calling to warn him. There was a murder in the building today. Cops were just by."

"Murder? Who cares?"

"Well, they asked if I had any visitors and I said you, in case someone saw you here…"

"Well, that was bright," Hans said sarcastically. "What'd you tell them I was there for?"

"I said you had some movie tickets for Disney and you brought them for Bobby."

"What would I do that for?" Hans questioned incredulously.

"You happened to get some tickets. I don't know how, some kind of prize or promotion, or maybe some poor sap you mugged, and who else do you know with a kid?"

"Gee, maybe my ma, Specs. Or maybe my girl. Think, why don't you?"

"How was I supposed to know? It seemed like a good reason to me."

"The only reason I'd give you tickets is if I wanted you to owe me for something. And what would I want from you, other than pictures? You obviously don't want them savvy to that scam," Hans pointed out.

Henry thought quickly. "A favor… like introducing you to a girl or something?"

"What girls do you know?" Hans jeered.

"I know girls. I do the teen parent thing at school. I'm the only guy in a class full of girls. And they've all been knocked up, so they must have something going for them. Some of them are pretty hot, and they're all friends with me because they figure I'm responsible."

Hans considered this in silence for a minute. "All right," he agreed finally. "I'll go for that if they show up. I gave you free tickets 'cause I want you to set me up with some hot chick you know."

"Okay," Henry was relieved that Hans had agreed to the story. "Thanks."

"Yeah. See you later."

———

Henry was fast asleep when a pounding on the door awoke him. He got up groggily, rubbing his eyes. It couldn't be the cops;

how would they already be on his trail? He put on his glasses and opened the door a crack. Hoods. More of Marty's boys, or was this something new? Henry was cautious and kept the chain on.

"Who is it?" His voice was hoarse.

They didn't appear to be in the mood for conversation. One of them put his shoulder to the door, snapping the chain and smashing the door into Henry's face.

"Ow!" Henry fell back, rubbing his cheekbone. "What're you trying to do?"

They grabbed him roughly, grunting and growling. Henry frantically tried to pull away.

"What's this about? Come on—I got a baby to look after, just tell me what you want!"

"You come, or we drag you," one of them growled, hauling on Henry's arm. They were two big bruisers, and Henry had no doubt they were packing weapons too.

"I can't leave the baby alone," Henry said, a bit of a whine creeping into his voice. He had just woken up, his face hurt, and he hated to be bullied.

"Listen." One of them stuck his face right in front of Henry's. "You're coming. If you're gonna cause trouble, you're gonna be sorry. Now, what's it gonna be?"

"I just don't—" Henry started to protest again, and the big hood hauled off and hit him. A closed fist, not an open hand, right in the nose.

Henry yelped. His knees buckled with the pain. Bright lights and dark spots danced in front of his eyes. He swore, tears welling up and overflowing down his cheeks. They dragged him out of the apartment and down the hall. They didn't bother trying to negotiate the stairs with him struggling between them. They just pushed him down the first flight. Henry staggered to his feet on the landing, breathing heavily. He didn't have to be told they'd throw him down the next flight if he didn't co-operate.

He held the handrail and unsteadily went down the remaining two flights on his feet. The two thugs grabbed him again at the bottom and dragged him out to a car. He was pushed into the back seat and driven somewhere not too far away, and taken down to the basement of some building.

Hans was there, along with a couple of other gang members. The thugs let go of Henry. He held his face, feeling the puffiness of his nose.

"That goon broke my nose," Henry complained. He knew it was broken. That grating and the pain gave it away. It wasn't the first time. A football accident, he'd told his teacher at the time. Henry's eyes were still swimming with tears and he was swallowing putrid blood from his nose. He tried to lean forward so it would drip down his face instead of down his throat.

"Did I tell you to rough him up?" Hans demanded. "If anyone asks, you just tell 'em you got mugged." Hans told Henry.

Henry sniffled. "You told them to bring me? Why didn't you just come to see me in the morning?"

"I can't afford to be seen there. You already told them I was there, so they'll suspect me first."

"Suspect you of what?"

"Richie's murder."

"Richie was murdered too?" Henry allowed a couple of beats to connect it up. "What—you mean he was the one killed in my building?" he asked incredulously.

"Like you didn't already know that," Hans growled.

"How would I know?"

"You think I'm gonna think it was the girl? You're the one that killed him. What for? Because of the pictures? I just don't get it!"

"What girl?" Henry questioned. His mind was still reeling and Hans wasn't making much sense. The girl? What did a girl have to do with Richie's murder?

"The girl Richie saw before you, Specs. You stoned or what?"

That girl.

"I just woke up, got hit in the face, and thrown down the stairs," Henry snapped. "Sorry if I'm a little groggy!"

Hans walked closer to him. "Why'd you do it? Huh? What'd Richie ever do to you to deserve that?"

"I didn't even see him. He never showed up!"

"You're lying. He left the girl's place, went up to see you, and you took him down to the basement and killed him!" Hans accused.

"Why would I take him to the basement?" Henry demanded.

"To kill him!"

"Why would he go with me?"

Hans frowned. He looked at the other guys. Henry wondered what they were. Lieutenants? Advisers? Observers? More thugs? They just looked at Hans and said nothing.

Hans couldn't answer Henry's question. Why would Richie go down to the basement with him? There was no logical explanation.

"He'd only go with someone he trusted," Henry suggested. "Like someone from the gang."

"You trying to frame me? You tell the cops I was there and then you say it was someone from the gang? What're you trying to do?" Hans said frantically.

"You're trying to implicate me," Henry pointed out. "I didn't kill anyone. I don't even own a gun."

"A gun?" Hans repeated blankly. "Who said anything about a gun?"

"I just figured, you know, gang banger gets killed, it's usually a shooting."

Again, Hans exchanged looks with the observers in consternation. He pulled a knife out of his pocket and switched it open.

"Just who do you think you're messing with, Specs?" He put the tip of the knife against Henry's throat. "Don't think you can pull the wool over my eyes. You are gonna tell me what happened. Everything. And why. And maybe then I'll turn you over to the cops and not kill you right here."

Henry swallowed. "I never killed anyone," he said evenly. "How would I kill a professional like Richie? How many guys have tried before? He's savvy, he's suspicious. How does a geek like me overcome a guy like that?"

The blade bit into him. In a reflex motion, Henry raised his hand to push it away. The two thugs that had brought him in jumped forward and grabbed him. They twisted Henry's arm painfully hard behind his back, making him cry out.

"I didn't have anything to do with it! Just let me go."

"Tell me what you did," Hans insisted.

"Nothing! I waited for him. He never showed up. You came and I finished the deal with you."

Hans hit him, the knife in his hand. Everything swam before Henry's eyes.

40

Henry woke up with his face on the pavement. He wasn't sure how he had gotten there or where exactly he was. A strong hand was shaking his shoulder.

"Come on, get up there," a voice urged gruffly. "Get off the doorstep."

Henry rolled over groggily. He tried to grip the concrete with his hands to keep the world from spinning out of control. It was useless.

"Get up, kid."

His whole body screamed with pain. He groaned a protest.

"Let's get you on your feet."

Henry tried to get up, strong hands helping him to his feet. He leaned against the rough brick building, sobbing and trying to swim out of the pain and back to the outside world. He could process only disjointed images. It was still night. Big fingers grasped his chin, turning his head until blinding light ripped through his brain. Henry moaned.

"It's him," the voice said.

Great. Someone else who was looking for him.

"Can you make it up the stairs to your apartment?"

Henry shook his head hopelessly, tears streaming down his

face from the pain and the bright light. The light moved out of his eyes. Henry's nose was either running or still bleeding. He sniffled, trying not to sob aloud.

"Come here. Sit down."

He was guided to the steps and lowered into a sitting position. The men waited quietly for him to settle down. Henry breathed deeply, trying to calm the pain. He tried to stop his body from shaking and shuddering. Even breathing deeply hurt. Eventually, Henry raised his head from his hands to see who the men were. Dawson and Cruz, the cops. Henry swore and lowered his head again.

"You wanna tell us what happened?" Dawson questioned.

"Got mugged," Henry groaned, going with the first thing that came to his mind. The story that Hans said to use.

"Or maybe Hans found out you put him in the building and sent some goons after you," Cruz commented.

Henry didn't answer this.

"You should see a doctor," Dawson said.

"Yeah," Henry agreed.

"You want us to take you to the clinic or the hospital?"

Henry nodded. He swallowed, trying to steady his voice. "Bobby—he's alone."

"Your son?" Cruz questioned.

"Yeah."

"I'll go get him. Where's your keys?"

Henry felt his pockets, then found he was wearing his pajamas and had no keys or wallet with him.

"I don't have them. Maybe the super…? It might still be unlocked. Oh—what if it's unlocked, and someone could go in there—"

"Don't panic," Dawson soothed. "Cruz will go up and get him right now. He'll break down the door if he has to."

Henry rested his head in his hands while he waited. His mind drifted, and he had to be shaken awake again when Cruz returned.

"I got Bobby. He's safe," Cruz said. "The door was unlocked, but it was shut. No one has been in there, judging by the fact that your TV was still there."

Henry whispered a brief prayer of thanks.

"Let's get you to a doctor now."

"Yeah," Henry agreed. Dawson put a strong arm around Henry's waist, pulling him to his feet. Henry groaned, fighting the pain and trying to stay conscious.

He blacked out somewhere between the building and the car.

It didn't hurt so much when Henry woke up again. His head was foggy, thick with painkillers. He felt his bruised face with cautious fingers. It was badly swollen, tender even through the narcotics. His broken nose had been set.

"How do you feel?" a voice questioned.

Henry turned his head slowly. Dawson was sitting in a chair beside him, rubbing the bridge of his nose in a tired gesture.

"Sore, Woozy."

"I bet," Dawson agreed, "you look like a prizefighter."

Henry looked for a mirror. There were bruises on his arms, which were lying on top of the sheets.

"What did they do to you?" Dawson questioned.

Henry didn't know what to say. Was he supposed to stick to the mugging story? Hadn't Dawson already guessed it was Hans?

"Where's Bobby?" he asked, stalling.

"He's okay. There's a daycare."

"Good."

"You're black and blue from head to toe. It's obvious it was the gang. What exactly did they do?"

"Threw me down the stairs, for starters," Henry said.

"Yep, that's exactly what it looks like. What'd they want from you?"

"Nothing."

"Just didn't like you putting Hans in the building?"

"I dunno."

"Come on. You're not in trouble. If the gang did this to you for saying Hans was around, there's good reason to think that Hans has something to hide. Don't you think?" Dawson coaxed.

"I don't know."

"So you're going to let him get away with it?"

Henry nodded. He closed his eyes and fell back asleep.

———

Henry was more sore after going home than he had been at the hospital. The drugs they gave him to take home were not nearly as strong as those he had been on. He hobbled around stiffly, stopping to rest every minute or two. Sometimes when he stopped to rest, he couldn't get himself moving again for another hour or more. His body felt like a lump of molten lead. Fiery with pain. Too heavy to drag around.

The super grudgingly fixed the chain on his door. As he worked, he gossiped about the police and the body found in the basement. Henry fed Bobby some cut up apples for supper and put him in his crib, hoping to get to bed early. There was a knock on the door. Henry's heart started beating hard. He went to the door, breaking out in a cold sweat.

"Who's there?" he asked through the door. He wasn't going to take the chance of opening the door this time, even with the chain on. He wished there was a peephole.

"It's Sandy."

Henry opened the door cautiously with the chain on to make sure that it was her. He saw her and took the chain off.

"Hi."

She walked in and went into the kitchen. "I heard about

your trouble with John's gang." She looked him over. "You're an awful mess."

"I know."

She started cleaning up the mess in the kitchen that Henry hadn't had the energy to work on. Henry opened his mouth to protest, then changed his mind and sank into the armchair. He watched her, exhausted.

"Did you have something to eat?" Sandy asked.

"No appetite."

"You have to have something." She looked through cupboards. "Will you eat mac and cheese?"

"There's no milk."

"I can make it without. We'll just add something else to it." She checked the fridge. "Salsa?"

"Sure."

Sandy continued to clean up while cooking his dinner. She handed him the pasta in a bowl with a fork and studied his face.

"You due for some meds before bed?" she suggested.

"Yeah."

"Where are they?"

"Bathroom."

She disappeared for a moment and came back, turning the bottle in her hand and frowning. "Is this it?" she questioned doubtfully.

"Yeah."

"But this is just Tylenol. It won't even take the edge off."

"That's all they'd give me."

Sandy shook her head in disgust. "I'll get you something stronger. Let's get you in bed first so you'll be more comfortable."

She helped lift him out of the chair and, putting her arm around his waist and his around her shoulders, helped him totter like an old man to the bedroom. She pulled the sheets back and gently lowered him down. Rather than just leaving him like that, she unlaced his shoes and took off his socks and shoes. He thought she would stop there, but she reached for the fastener on his pants.

"No, don't," Henry protested, pushing her away.

"Oh, don't get all squirmy on me," she snapped. "Nothin' here I don't see a hundred times a day."

Henry met her frank, steady gaze and relented. He let her hand go. She unfastened his jeans and pulled them off. She left his t-shirt on and pulled up the sheets.

"Now you lay still and hang in there. I'll be right back with something good." She looked around. "Where's your keys?"

Henry tapped his chest. She pulled the chain with the key on it out from under his shirt.

"I'll lock up so you and Bobby are safe and let myself back in."

"Okay."

She left. The apartment was quiet. The weight of his pain and the fatigue grew heavier. He could hear nothing but the beating of his heart and the ticking of the clock on his bedside table. Time crawled by and the pain grew. Maybe Sandy wasn't coming back. Maybe she had been distracted, intercepted, or arrested. The only painkillers he had in the house were the Tylenol Sandy had left in the front room. They were better than nothing. He could take a handful of them and maybe get some sleep.

Henry crawled out of bed. It was easier to stay on all fours than to climb to his feet. He dragged himself along, the pain growing with every movement.

41

————

Henry had blacked out in the hall. He woke up, feverish and covered with sweat. His body was racked with pain. Sandy lifted his head.

"I told you to stay put! Can't guys ever do what they're told?" she griped. She stroked his hair for a minute. "Can you get up? If I help you?"

Henry just moaned in pain.

"Okay. Just lie still."

She set his head back down gently. He wasn't sure what she was doing. He felt a constriction around his arm, then coldness. There was a needle prick, followed by a rush of warmth. Henry's head started to spin. For a few minutes, he was lost in a whirlpool of nausea and pain, and then slowly, the pain receded. He began to drift off to sleep, finally comfortable. Sandy roused him.

"That taking? You're looking a bit better."

"Yeah. What was it?"

"Morphine."

"Wow."

"Let's get you up and into your bed."

"Okay."

She helped him to his feet and steadied him as he swayed. She walked him back to the bedroom and laid him down again.

"You're a good nurse," he told her.

She looked surprised and laughed. "A nurse, right."

"You are. You're great."

"You're off your head. You go to sleep now. I'll sleep on the couch in case you or Bobby need something."

"Okay."

Henry closed his eyes and quickly swirled down through the darkness into sleep.

———

When he awoke in the morning, Sandy sat on the side of the bed and gave him another shot. This time he was aware enough to watch her put an efficient tourniquet on his arm, swab his skin, and inject the morphine. She watched his face for changes and stroked his hair comfortingly.

"What's broken, other than your nose?"

"Ribs, a hairline fracture in my arm. They said it didn't need to be set. That's all they said."

"You have at least three broken bones and they sent you home without codeine?"

"Yeah."

"And they wonder why poor slobs go to street drugs. How long were you in the hospital?"

"Two days."

"And they released you 'cause you got no insurance."

"Yeah, I guess."

She swore and shook her head. "I gotta go take care of some business. You know how to do this?" she gestured to the syringes on the table.

"I've never done it..." Henry trailed off.

"It isn't hard," she said with a shrug. "You'll do it if you need it."

"How often can I take it?"

"Whenever you need it."

Henry nodded, wondering whether he would be able to inject himself. He wasn't fond of needles.

"Thanks for coming last night," he told her. "I really needed help."

She seemed embarrassed by his thanks. "No sweat. I'll see you in a bit, okay?"

———

Henry waited until the pain got bad again, but not so long that his hands wouldn't be steady. Sandy was right about him learning pretty quickly to do it by himself. It was just a question of need. The pain of the jabs wasn't nearly as bad as the pain if he didn't take it. It wasn't long before he could hit the vein on the first try nearly every time. Sandy checked in on him each night and stayed in case Bobby needed her. He wondered how she could spend so much time at his place without her business suffering.

"I thought I wasn't your type," he reminded her one day, when he was feeling good after a shot.

She eyed him. "You're not. But if John's gang is that upset with you, ya can't be all bad." She gave him a wry smile.

"Did he say anything to you about me?"

"John? He doesn't talk to me."

"Oh. He hasn't called me in the last little while. Since—you know."

"Maybe he won't."

"What do the cops think about Richie? Are they going to arrest Hans?" Henry realized that he was chattering on. But Sandy didn't seem to mind.

"I dunno. Last I heard, they were investigating him and Katya," she said.

"Katya?"

"A girl Richie saw that day. They think maybe her and Hans were in on it together."

"What do you think?"

"I don't really care. The guy was a leech. The neighborhood is better off without him."

Henry nodded thoughtfully.

"You should be weaning yourself off the morphine," Sandy commented. "You're healing up."

"I *am*," Henry protested. "I'm not taking it very often."

"You're high right now."

Henry was startled. He hadn't shot up in front of her in days. He didn't think anyone could tell. It was only morphine; it didn't make him behave any differently.

"You think that I haven't seen enough junkies to be able to tell?" Sandy challenged. "You're not hiding it from anyone who has any experience."

"How can you tell?" Henry questioned.

"Your eyes. The expression on your face."

"I just took a little to settle the pain."

"You're hooked. If you don't quit now, you're going to be in trouble."

"I'm not hooked," he immediately protested. "Once my bones finish mending—"

"You're hooked. Admit it and deal with it. I'm not bringing you any more," she said flatly.

Henry swallowed. No more? That was it? She was just going to cut him off like that, without any warning? He would have stockpiled it a bit, had he known, so that he could wean himself off slowly. How was that any different than the hospital releasing him just with Tylenol?

"Fine," he agreed, with a shrug. "I can probably dial back to Tylenol now."

"Yeah. OTC's now. You're getting better."

———

Henry wasn't paying enough attention to his surroundings and didn't see Hans until the boy stepped right in front of him. It was too late to cross the street or avoid him. Henry just stopped and stood there, his heart sinking, wondering what fresh torture he was in for now.

"Hey, Specs," Hans said coolly, looking him up and down.

Henry licked dry lips. His heart raced. He didn't know what to do. "Hey," he said weakly.

"You know, I been meaning to come see you."

"I didn't say anything to anyone—"

Hans waved his hand. "No, no. Not that. Those last pictures you took, they weren't half bad. I got some more for you to do."

He looked at Henry expectantly.

"I don't want any more jobs like that," Henry growled.

"I ain't asking, just like Richie didn't ask. You'll do the jobs I give you."

Henry gritted his teeth and didn't argue further. He swallowed and took a deep breath, shoving his hands into his pockets. "I need something..."

"What do I care what you need?" Hans questioned.

"I just thought you might know where..." Henry couldn't go on. He stopped, swallowing.

"What do you want?" Hans asked.

"Some morphine."

Hans laughed. "Morphine! I don't think so. You don't get pure morphine on the street. Maybe something else cut with morphine. Coke or heroin."

"I don't want coke, just morphine. For pain."

"I'll see what I can find you, buddy-boy. But I can't guarantee purity."

Henry nodded. "Soon?"

"Soon as you get me some pictures."

Hans gave Henry the directions for the next shoot.

———

Henry hung the prints shakily and looked at his watch. He had already called Hans looking for his morphine. He was in terrible pain, sweating and shaking, hardly able to catch his breath. There was a knock on the door and Henry ran to answer it. It was Hans, with someone else from the gang that Henry didn't know. Henry paid him no attention.

"Did you get it?" Henry questioned.

"Sure," Hans assured him calmly. "Where's the pics?"

"In the darkroom, just drying."

Hans took his time checking them out. Henry pushed the negatives at him, sweating heavily. Hans delved into his pocket and pulled out the drugs.

"Don't take too much," he advised. "You can always take more after, but if you OD on this, you're toast."

Henry steadied his hands and gave himself a shot. The shakes started to calm and warmth and well-being flooded over him. He let his breath out in a long sigh. Once he began to relax, he noticed he felt different from when he took morphine. He felt… good. Pumped. Energized. He grinned, his anxieties about Hans and his buddy being in the apartment disappearing.

"What's in that?" he questioned.

Hans shrugged. "Bit of this, bit of that. Mostly heroin."

"Really? I thought heroin made you feel bad.'

"Would people take it if it made you feel bad? You take it because it makes you feel good," Hans pointed out.

"Well, I'm just taking it for the pain. When my bones are healed, that's it."

Hans chuckled. "Yeah. Sure, Specs."

"How much…?" Henry was embarrassed to ask. "How much does this cost?"

"I'll give it to you for the cost of the photo job. The pictures for the drugs."

"Okay."

That was easy enough. The shoot only took an hour, and he had enough of the narcotics for a few days. If he still needed more after that, one more photoshoot would cover him until he was healed.

42

─────────

Henry had missed a lot of school. He felt awkward going back there and sitting at his desk as if nothing had happened. He sat down, trying to look calm and unconcerned, while inside, his heart pounded. Mrs. Clark came over to him.

"Hi, Henry. How're you doing?" she questioned sympathetically.

"Still a little rough," Henry admitted.

"You don't look too good."

"Yeah. But I can't miss too much."

"We're glad to have you back. But take it easy. Okay?"

Henry nodded. "I will."

He had a pretty tough time making it through the day. At lunchtime, he went into the restroom and shot up. He sat on the can, breathing deeply and feeling the pain wash away. Someone else came in, so Henry quickly flushed the toilet and left.

He hadn't brought lunch and he had no appetite. He went into the library instead of the cafeteria and looked for something to occupy his mind. He found a book, but couldn't concentrate on it. He was hyped up, his mind going a mile a minute. He needed to walk, run, something. He was too jumped up to sit still and think.

"Henry—"

Henry nearly jumped out of his skin at the hand on his shoulder. "What?"

He turned and saw Cherie, one of the girls in his class, smiling expectantly at him.

"Man, I'm sorry. I didn't mean to scare you," Cherie apologized.

Henry laughed, putting his hand over his racing heart. "It's okay, I'm all right. You scared the wits out of me!"

She was mortified. "I'm so sorry—I know you got mugged and all. I should have been more careful."

Henry took a deep breath and gave her a little hug. "It's okay. Really. I'm all right."

"Are you sure?"

"Yeah. I'm fine. Let's go for a walk."

Cherie looked surprised. "Umm—sure."

They left the school and struck off towards the mall.

"So, how are you doing?" Cherie inquired.

"Rough. I just took a painkiller, though, so I'm okay for a while."

"You poor guy. I can't imagine how awful it must have been."

Henry nodded. "It wasn't fun," he agreed.

"You gotta move out of that neighborhood. It's too dangerous."

"There's nowhere else that I can afford," Henry pointed out, "it's subsidized."

"They won't move you when you get mugged and beaten?" she demanded incredulously.

"There was even a murder in my building. The cops came and questioned me!"

"No way. You gotta get yourself out of there."

"Yeah," Henry agreed.

"I'd be scared to leave my apartment, even in the daytime."

"You can't think about it. The gangs, drugs, muggings, murders—you can't spend your time thinking about all that."

"How can you be mugged yourself and not think about it?"

Henry shrugged. "I don't know. I have to think about school, and Bobby, and how to take care of us."

"Wow."

"Let's talk about something else. What's been going on while I was gone?"

Cherie considered, and then went into a narrative of what had happened lately. They didn't go back to classes in the afternoon.

———

"Are you doing all right?" the daycare teacher asked Henry when he picked up Bobby. "They said you missed classes this afternoon."

"Yeah," Henry avoided meeting Cherie's eyes. "I had to go lie down."

Of course, lying down at Cherie's place hadn't had anything to do with his not feeling well.

"You take care of yourself. This little sweetie depends on you."

"Was he good?" Henry questioned. "I didn't know how he'd be, after being away for so long."

"A little fussy," she assured him. "I'm sure he'll settle right back in."

"Yeah. Good."

They took Bobby out into the hallway, and Cherie giggled. "I didn't mean to get you in trouble."

"I'm not in trouble, don't worry about it."

———

When he eventually returned home, in need of at least a change of clothes, Henry was surprised to find Sandy in his apartment.

"Sandy? What are you doing here?"

"Better question—where have you been the past three days?" she countered.

Henry shrugged. "Out. But what are you doing here?" he persisted.

"Worrying about what happened to you! You disappear without a word to anyone; I don't know if you've run into Hans or John or something—"

"John?" Henry repeated. "Marty?"

"Yeah, Marty," she said impatiently. "How was anyone supposed to know where you were?"

"When did Marty get out? How did he get out so soon?" Henry demanded, his heart racing as he thought of running into Marty again. This was not good.

"I don't know the details," Sandy said coolly.

"I was just with a friend," Henry said finally. "Nothing happened to me."

"Nice of you to let someone know what was going on," she sneered sarcastically.

"I didn't know I had to report to you."

They faced off against each other, both self-righteous and defensive.

"How did you get in?" Henry demanded.

Sandy hesitated for a moment. "I copied your key when I borrowed it," she admitted, "in case…"

"You copied my key without asking?" Henry's voice rose several notes. "Took advantage because I was sick? I want it back."

Sandy took out her key chain and removed a key from it, tossing it onto the table.

"Fine. There you go. Don't expect any help from me if something happens to you."

Sandy tossed her long red hair and stormed out. Henry

watched her go, frowning. He should probably call her back. Apologize. But he was so angry about her demanding to know where he was and breaking into his apartment. That was wrong. She shouldn't have done that.

He was also embarrassed at having been at another girl's house. He had a feeling that despite what Sandy said about him not being her type, she had feelings for him. Maybe just motherly feelings because she'd nursed him when she was sick, but he couldn't just tell a girl who liked him that he had spent a few nights with another girl.

But as he cooled down, Henry realized he had bigger things to worry about. Marty was out of prison. How did he get out so soon after staging a prison uprising? Didn't that get a few years added to his sentence?

Maybe he'd escaped. In that case, all Henry had to do was call the cops. But if he was out legitimately… then what was Henry going to do then?

———

Henry tried not to be in the neighborhood too much, hoping to avoid running into Marty. He knew it was an exercise in futility, but he had to at least try to protect himself. He didn't want another encounter with the gang. But Marty caught him on the street one day in front of his building.

"Well, hey, Specs," he said cheerfully. "How's it going?"

Henry's heart pounded. He tried to swallow.

"M-marty."

"How're you doing, kid? Saw old Sandy the other day, and she was pretty steamed at you."

"We had a disagreement."

Mary chuckled. "Yeah, I figured. What was going on between you? You getting a little action there?"

Henry felt himself flush and Marty laughed.

"I hope you were careful, man. You never know where that one's been!"

Henry's face burned like it was on fire. He was sweating heavily. "How did you get out so fast?" he asked.

"There's ways and means you'll never know of," Marty said mysteriously.

"Oh."

"Say, I heard about what happened with you and my gang," Marty said. "These boys tend to be all brawn and no brain, you know what I mean? They just don't think things through."

Henry nodded wordlessly.

"I hope there's no hard feelings. I figure it was probably the girl Richie got himself tangled up with. We'll keep an eye on her."

Henry tried to figure out how to disengage from the conversation. He was relieved to be told there were no more hard feelings. But he still felt uncomfortable talking to Marty.

"We got more photo jobs for you," Marty said easily. "You up for it?"

"Yeah, sure," Henry agreed. There was no arguing over the jobs anymore. They were his source for a fix, and he still needed the drugs to get past the pain of his injuries.

"Good. I've been looking at your later work. Not bad."

Henry was fast learning how to get the pictures that Marty wanted quickly and efficiently, even from shy or reluctant models. He still hated the work and hardly even looked at the photos when he developed them. But he was just a little proud of his growing expertise. He shrugged off Marty's compliment modestly.

"I'll see you around," Marty said, walking away.

Henry leaned against the wall, his heart pounding. The pain in his broken bones was suddenly intense. He went back upstairs to shoot up.

43

Cherie rolled her eyes when Henry picked up his camera.

"No more pictures, Henry," she protested.

"Come on, just a couple," Henry coaxed, snapping one as she looked coyly up at him.

"What's the thing with you and cameras?" Cherie questioned.

She wasn't mad, though. She always fussed, but still let him take pictures.

"I like taking pictures and I like the way you look."

He changed his angle as she stretched lazily. She smiled at him. "You're always taking pictures, but never the kind I thought you would…"

Henry shrugged. He took enough of the other kind elsewhere. He liked Cherie's body, but had no desire to take nude pictures of her. Sometimes, like with Adrienne, he followed her and took candid shots of her. But he wasn't as infatuated with Cherie as he had been with Adrienne. Not yet, anyway.

"A couple more," he breathed, admiring the red sweater that clung snugly to her perfect curves. Cherie struck a couple of poses and he obligingly snapped them, but he knew that the pictures he kept would be the ones where she was relaxed and looked away from the camera.

———

Henry was watching Bobby playing in the playground. He had his camera around his neck and wondered how soon he could convince Bobby to go home. He saw Sandy down by the street and for a joke, raised his camera and snapped a picture of her. Sandy saw him and scowled. Henry snapped another shot. Sandy walked over.

"You want me to expose your film?" she threatened.

"No."

"Then don't take pictures of me."

"I didn't," he lied. "I was just joking."

"You better not. You keep away from me with your camera."

Henry shrugged. "Listen," he said uncertainly, "I'm sorry… about blowing up at you before. I just… I was just surprised to find you in my place."

"I was worried about you. Really worried. You never disappeared like that before."

"I know. I should have said thank you for caring, not have kicked you out like that. You can have the key back if you want."

She shook her head.

"If something ever did happen, I'd want someone to know. I'd want someone to come."

She shrugged, looking down. "I dunno. If you want."

"I do. Is that okay? I'm really sorry."

"Okay. Don't keep going on about it. It wasn't that big a deal."

Henry nodded.

Sandy took out a package of cigarettes and lit one, offering him the box with a small motion.

"No thanks. That's really not good for you," he commented.

Sandy looked at him, brows raised. "Oh, it's not good for me, huh? What about the stuff you're shooting?"

"That's just for…" he trailed off at the look in her eye. "Okay. I'm one to talk."

She nodded. "I told you that you were gonna get hooked and you wouldn't listen. You don't think I know what I'm talking about?"

"I know. I just… have a hard time admitting that you might know better. I mean, we're the same age. I think you can't know any better than me."

Sandy pushed up her sleeve, showing off arms riddled with needle tracks. "I know, okay? I try to stay away from the hard stuff now. Stick to rave drugs and cigarettes. But you can see what a good job I'm doing of that."

Henry stared at the ugly marks, feeling apprehension about his drug use for the first time. If he kept shooting up, his arms were going to look like that. They would look like that and he wouldn't be able to stop. Sandy pulled her sleeve back down slowly.

"My life ain't been like yours, Thomas."

"Thomson," Henry corrected automatically. He looked away from her. "What has your life been like? Marty says you usually live with your dad."

"I have my own place now. I used to live with my dad."

"Why not with your mom?"

"She never wanted me," she said with a shrug of her shoulders. "Da did. I guess he saw opportunities for profit."

"What do you mean?" Bobby started crying, and Henry went and picked him up. "Let's go back to my place. He needs a nap."

Sandy walked with him. When they got up to his apartment, she got a drink from the fridge and sat down.

"My dad's a businessman," she said, as if their conversation had not been interrupted ten minutes ago. "He looks for the profit in anything. Having a kid around, particularly a girl, most people wouldn't see that as a money-making opportunity. He found ways."

Henry tried to imagine what those ways would be. Some of them she had already hinted at or he knew about. The p-notes and prostitution. Who knew how young that had started? Maybe running drugs for him. The way she objected to Henry's taking pictures, she'd probably done kiddie porn too. There were probably dozens of other things she had done that he couldn't even imagine.

"Where is he now?"

"Prison. Where else?"

"What for?"

"Umm, bookmaking this time."

"For how long?"

"About a year. Usually, it's just for a few months. Not usually so long."

"You're not staying with your mom while he's there?"

"No. I just keep an eye on her when everyone else is in the clink."

"Was she married to your dad? They live together?"

"Not since I can remember. I've lived with her a few times, but we don't really get along."

Henry nodded. "Do you get along with your dad? I mean, with all of the stuff he made you do?"

Sandy smoothed her hair back and shrugged. "We get along. I dunno, he got me into a lot of stuff, and I guess I was too young to be able to say if I wanted to or not, but mostly he was good to me. He looked after me, didn't give me any trouble as long as I played it straight." She grinned. "He taught me a trade, taught me how to take care of myself and make good money."

Henry shook his head. "I don't know how you can joke about it."

"You can't take yourself seriously all the time."

"Yeah, but… it's not funny," Henry protested.

"Sure it is. Life's funny. You telling me nothing about your life is funny?"

"No."

Sandy shook her head. "You'll just end up in trouble if you can't laugh about yourself now and then."

Henry grunted. He looked at his watch. "I gotta go to the can. I'll be back in a second."

He left her and went into the bathroom, where he quickly tied a tourniquet on his arm. The door opened, making him jump, and for an instant, he tried to hide the tourniquet from her. "Hey! What are you doing?" he protested, embarrassed at being caught.

"I thought you were going to stop," she said, an eyebrow cocked questioningly.

Henry looked at his arm and at the syringe on the sink. "I can't," he admitted.

"You have to stop. We gotta dry you out."

"I can't ask for help. They'll take Bobby away."

"Find someone to look after him and check yourself in. That's responsible. They won't take him if you make proper arrangements."

"I don't know."

Sandy pointed to the syringe. "That or Bobby," she said flatly.

Henry knew in his heart that it had to be Bobby, but his body craved the drugs. He needed them. He didn't have to choose, not really. He'd wean himself off the heroin slowly. He'd look after Bobby. There was no need to tell anyone that he was taking heroin and take the chance of losing him. Henry reached for the syringe.

"I'll cut down slowly," he told her.

He intended to only take half of what was in the needle, but his thumb pushed the plunger in all the way. Sandy looked at him steadily.

"Do you disgust yourself?"

Henry felt the rush of the heroine. "Yes," he agreed, and just breathed, basking in the high.

44

Henry waited, nervously flipping through magazines without reading a word. Eventually, Dr. Denzel came out. He shook hands warmly.

"Hi, Henry. How's it going?" he greeted heartly.

"Okay."

"Come on in." The doctor gestured for him to enter.

Henry followed Denzel to his office.

"Saw your mom the other day," Denzel commented. "She's looking better."

Henry was stunned. His mouth went dry. "What?" he said blankly.

"Dorry's your mom, right?" Denzel glanced at Henry's new chart for verification. "She was in this week to renew her meds. Looked good."

"My mom disappeared months ago," Henry said hoarsely.

Denzel looked puzzled. "Disappeared?" he repeated.

"Just didn't come home one day... I figured she'd jumped off a bridge or something. I never thought... did she give you her new address?"

The doctor nodded. "Yes, of course... but I can't give it to you because of confidentiality."

They sat in silence, just contemplating this for a while.

"So that wasn't why you came today," the doctor said finally.

"No."

"Tell me what's on your mind," he invited.

"I... I need to be admitted."

"Okay. What's wrong?"

"I—um—I've been having some problems, and I—um..."

Henry just didn't know how to say it. He hated to admit that he had a drug problem. That things had gotten so bad. He tripped over the words. His mouth was so dry. He swallowed and tried again to speak.

"Try to relax, Henry," Dr. Denzel soothed. "Why don't you talk about your symptoms? Are you feeling depressed?"

"Sometimes."

"Anxious?"

"Yeah."

"How are you sleeping?" Denzel inquired.

"Not... not too well."

"School?"

"I've been missing... grades are down..."

"How are you eating? You look like you've lost weight recently."

Henry nodded. "Uh-huh."

"Drugs?"

Henry nodded.

"What drugs, Henry?"

Henry gulped. He licked his lips, rough and dry as sandpaper. This was it. "Heroin, mostly."

The doctor didn't act shocked. He nodded his head understandingly. "What do you think has triggered all this?"

Henry rolled his eyes. "A lot of things have happened. I've had trouble with the police. Mom leaving. Then I got beaten up and started on narcotics for the pain."

The doctor nodded slowly. "I thought I could get in here, maybe, since this is where Ma always came," Henry explained.

"With the regular detox programs… the waiting lists are months long. I have to get dried out soon, before I get more addicted."

"I agree. You have a lot of risk factors. Your age, your mother's genes, the stress that you've been through. We don't know how much of this problem is drugs and what might be an emerging disorder like bipolar or schizophrenia. I want to get you evaluated as soon as possible."

"Okay." Henry let out his breath, relieved. "Good."

It was all going to be okay.

———

Henry paced across the room nervously. He had unpacked his few belongings into the drawers in the room, and there was nothing to do but wait. It was too quiet. In prison, it had always been too noisy. People talking, arguing, shouting. All of the noise from the whole cell block slicing through the bars of the cells. But in the tiny rooms of the clinic, everything was muffled. Muted. Smothered. Even yelling sounded far away and unreal.

His skin crawled, and he was sweating again. He wanted more heroin. Sandy had packed his bag for him to be sure that he couldn't smuggle something in. The clinic had checked his bag on arrival too. He was going to have to dry out.

———

"Henry. Henry."

Henry focused on Dr. Denzel's insistent voice, and he tried to concentrate. He looked across the desk at the doctor and stared at the center of his face.

"Sorry," he apologized, "I guess I was daydreaming."

"That's all right," the doctor said calmly. "Why don't you tell me what you were daydreaming about?"

"I don't know. I just sort of… phased out."

"Is that something you do often? Or just when you're in withdrawal?"

Henry's eyes wandered to the doctor's desk lamp, trying to stay focused and present.

"It's not just the withdrawal," he admitted.

"Tell me about it."

Henry thought back to his time in prison.

"I get overwhelmed… and I sort of… escape…"

"Uh-huh."

"I can't think and sort through everything."

"Is that how you feel right now?"

"Yeah."

"Tell me as many words as you can to describe how you feel."

"Overwhelmed… stressed… anxious…" Henry held his head between his hands. "I don't know. Drowning. Lost. Helpless."

"What's making you feel this way?" Denton asked.

"I don't know."

"What are you worrying about?"

"Bobby. Staying off drugs. Not staying off drugs. Being closed in. I don't know… I don't want to think about it."

"Why don't you want to think about it?"

"It's… too hard. I just want to hide. Withdraw."

The doctor was silent for a few minutes. "I want you to try a relaxation exercise with me. Close your eyes, and think of a place…"

Henry drifted.

———

"What do you do to relax, Henry?" Dr. Denzel questioned.

Henry felt better than he had previously, looser and relaxed, on a new medication to control his anxiety. He didn't feel shut down. He felt free-floating, more like an observer.

"I dunno. I don't have a lot of time," he said.

"You have any hobbies?"

"Photography."

"You like to take pictures?"

"Yeah."

"What kind?" Dr. Denzel prompted.

"People."

"Portraits?"

"No, not posed. More like candids."

"What else? Any other hobbies?"

"No."

Dr. Denzel took a few minutes to make notes on his file, letting him think about his answers. "How about your friends? Do you spend time with them?"

"Some, not a lot. I'm sort of a loner."

"Girlfriends?"

"Sometimes. I'm always surprised when girls are interested in me," Henry chuckled a bit.

"Why is that?"

"I'm not good looking, or popular, or a jock..." Henry shrugged.

"Are those the only ways to get a girl?"

"I guess not—I don't know why they're interested in me."

"Sounds like you've had some experience."

"I guess, yeah."

"Intimate?"

"Some," Henry admitted.

"Anyone serious?"

"There has been. Right now... not really. Just casual."

"How did the serious relationships end?"

Lana. Adrienne. Both dead. And Liz, though that wasn't serious, just spur of the moment.

"I—they just ended."

He saw their faces. Their fear at the last moment. The moment just before the end.

"Who ended them?"

"What?" Henry panicked, confused by the images. "Who killed them?"

There was silence. The doctor studied him levelly. "Who killed them, Henry?" Dr. Denzel repeated quietly.

"I don't know," Henry protested. "It wasn't me. No one ever proved it was me."

"But you did, didn't you?"

Henry shook his head in answer.

"Tell me about it," Denzel coaxed.

"It's private."

"Everything between us is private. You know I can't talk about it."

Henry avoided Denzel's eyes and stared out the window. "You'll think I'm an awful person," he said, "a monster."

"You're a patient looking for help. I don't judge you."

"Things just happen to me," Henry explained, shaking his head in confusion. "I don't go looking for trouble."

"Yes."

"Things just happen."

"Tell me about it, Henry, get it off your chest."

Henry hesitated, but the medications made it difficult to keep anything in. The words and emotions just bubbled up to the surface despite any initial misgivings, just bubbled up and out.

———

Henry looked at the pills that came with his dinner tray.

"These are different," he told the nurse.

"The doctor said he thought you were having more symptoms with the last protocol; he's changed them up again."

"Oh, okay." Henry took them obediently.

———

Henry looked around the doctor's office and jiggled his leg anxiously.

"Do you remember what we talked about last time?" Denzel questioned casually.

Henry avoided his eyes, looking at the floor. "No," he lied carefully. "It's all sort of foggy. Like I was dreaming or something." The medication he'd been on that day made him too talkative, took away too much control. He had to be on his guard in the future, more careful of what effect the meds might have on him.

"Sometimes, these drugs can affect you the wrong way," Denzel commented. "Instead of calming your symptoms, they can aggravate them. Make you more anxious, for example, or make you hallucinate or lose your sense of reality."

"Do you think that happened to me?"

"You were very different last session," Denzel diverted. "Not like yourself at all."

"What did I say?" Henry questioned. It was risky, but he wanted to know what Denzel's intentions were.

Dr. Denzel did not answer right away, studying Henry seriously. "You don't remember any of it?"

"No."

"Well, I think it's best that we just let it go and not pursue that line any further."

Henry breathed out slowly. "You think the meds made me hallucinate?"

"Those particular ones, yes. You seem okay on the current cocktail. How do you feel?"

Henry shrugged. He didn't feel good. But better to be a little anxious, even paranoid, than to risk another change that might make him say things he would later regret. "Okay, I guess. Better than before."

"Good. I want to make sure we have you stabilized before you are released."

Henry nodded. He stared out the window for a while. "What's my diagnosis?" he said suddenly.

Dr. Denzel looked surprised. "Of course. Well, as far as we can tell from your sessions and tests, some mild schizophrenia. With your mom's bipolar problems, I think you lean a little in that direction as well. You also show the beginnings of obsessive behavior. This is all very mild, easily controlled with some therapy and medication."

Henry nodded. "Okay."

Mild. Easily controlled. That all sounded good.

45

———

Sandy came to pick Henry up from the clinic when he was given a clean bill of health and released. She smiled and gave him a friendly hug and a peck on the cheek.

"Hey, Thomas. How's it going?"

Henry picked up his bag and got into the car without a word. Sandy got in and looked at him.

"No hello? What's with you?" she questioned, brows drawn down.

"Get me out of here," Henry growled.

Sandy looked suspicious. "You really dried out? You sound strung out."

Henry was irritated. "I don't want to be here. I'm not high. I just have to get out of here."

Sandy started the car and pulled out. She kept glancing over at Henry every couple of minutes. "So, how are you?" she prompted. "Feel good to be dry?"

Henry ignored her, staring out the window. "Come on, Thomas? What's going on? You're worse coming out than going in."

"Just let me be. I don't want to talk."

Sandy shook her head. "I'm doing you a favor. You can at least be civil."

"Yeah. Thank you. Now let me think."

He pressed his fingers to his temples. Sandy stayed quiet for a few minutes. A few times, she looked like she was going to say something but changed her mind. They pulled up to Henry's building. Henry opened the door and got out.

"Thanks," he said curtly, and shut the door before she could say anything else. He went up to the apartment and shut his door. He put the chain on, though he knew it wasn't real protection. He went into his room, crawled into the bed, and pulled the blankets over his head.

———

The days were a blur of nightmares. Henry couldn't go out. He was too anxious. Half the time, he couldn't even get out of bed. Sandy came by regularly, tried to talk to him and get him to go out. She sometimes brought groceries for him.

"What about Bobby?" Sandy prodded. "Don't you want to take care of him?"

"I can't take care of him now," Henry said flatly. He couldn't take care of himself, let alone a baby. He knew from Dorry's experience what happened when someone who couldn't cope tried to take care of a kid.

"You have to get straightened back out, so you can," Sandy told him. "Get yourself help so you can manage it again."

"Did you lock the door?" Henry questioned, though he was sure that she had. He went and checked just to be sure. "How long are you going to stay here?"

"What, am I disturbing your nap time?" she questioned sarcastically.

"I don't sleep anymore."

Though it was true that he spent much of his time in bed, he wasn't sleeping. He'd lie awake most of the night. He just felt safer there, under his covers, like a little kid hiding from the monsters under the bed or the clown in the closet.

"You need help, Thomas," Sandy said reasonably.

"No, I don't. I don't need anyone's help."

"You told me once your mom had emotional problems. Is this how she got?"

"She'd get depressed. I'm not depressed."

"Do you like the way you feel?"

"I don't need help," Henry reasserted, not about to be trapped by her logic. "I think you should go now."

Sandy looked at him for a long moment. She picked up her jacket and left.

———

Eventually, Henry's medications ran out. He couldn't convince himself to leave the apartment to get his prescription refilled. When Sandy came next, he handed her the empty bottle.

"Can you pick up my refill?"

Sandy shook her head. "No," she refused. "Not unless you go see your doctor."

"I get refills without a new prescription. It's right on the bottle."

"Don't care. I want the doctor to see you, know how this is affecting you."

Henry scowled at her. "Fine, I'll go get it refilled myself."

"Yeah? You're just gonna walk out that door and get it refilled?" Sandy asked sarcastically.

"That's right."

"Prove it. Go ahead, do it."

Henry walked over to the door and put his hand on the knob. He started to sweat, his scalp burning and heart racing. He compulsively checked the lock and chain.

"I don't feel like going out right now," he told Sandy weakly, leaning on the door for support.

"You can't, can you?"

"I'll go out later."

"Let someone help you, why don't you? You're a mess. Admit it. You can't do any of the things you used to like. Taking care of Bobby, going to school, even your stupid photography. You're not taking pictures any more at all, are you? What are you going to photograph, the locked door? And what about that blond at school you pretend I don't know about? Haven't seen her lately, have you?"

"If you're not going to help me, then just leave, all right?" Henry demanded, stung. "Please just leave."

Sandy headed for the door. "You know my number. I'm not coming back unless I hear from you. When you decide you're ready to go to the doctor and get some help, let me know."

She slammed the door and was gone. Henry watched the closed door for a moment, then locked and chained it. He went into the bathroom/darkroom and took a box of photos from the cupboard. Then he crawled into bed and pulled the blanket over his head. By the daylight that filtered through the blanket, he went through the pictures. Bobby, sweet Bobby who he could no longer take care of. Some interesting architecture. Shots down by the river carefully framed to exclude the garbage, drug paraphernalia, and urban sprawl. Candids he had snapped of Sandy, both casual and at work on the street. Pictures of Cherise, some of them smiling coyly at the camera and some taken while she was relaxed, unposed. His old life. The life he used to have. It wasn't fair. It wasn't fair that he should have to suffer this way.

He went to sleep without having taken any medication all day. Somehow, he would have to get more. He just couldn't face life without some help.

———

Maybe looking at his life like that had crystallized things. When Henry woke up in the morning, he felt clear-headed and somehow lighter. As if someone had tuned the radio in his head from static to a clear station.

He was hungry and made breakfast. He hadn't been hungry for a long time, eating like an automaton because the clock or Sandy said he ought to. Suddenly the food tasted real instead of like cardboard.

Henry put his empty prescription bottle into his pocket, put on his jacket, and cheerfully went out to get it refilled.

But the next morning, the cotton was back. The static was back. The anxiety was back. Henry was crushed. It was worse than before. The memory of that one clear day was torture. He stayed under the blanket all day. He wished that he had the courage to just die.

Sandy had said that she wouldn't come back unless Henry called her. He didn't. She left a series of messages on his machine. Henry strictly rationed what food he had left. When it was gone, he would either starve or get desperate enough to go out.

Sandy's increasingly worried messages filled up the tape so that it just beeped annoyingly when anyone called. Then Sandy came. She had a key, but the chain was still on, and she couldn't get in.

"Thomson, open the door. It's me!"

"I thought you weren't coming back," Henry reminded her.

"Why wouldn't you answer my calls? I've been worried sick."

Henry took the chain off. Behind Sandy stood Dr. Denzel. Henry stood there for a moment, then stepped back to let them both in without a word.

"How are you doing, Henry?" Dr. Denzel questioned.

"I'm okay."

Sandy and the doctor looked around the apartment. "You got food?" Sandy asked.

"For another day or two."

"Where'd you get food?"

"I went out."

"You went out?" she repeated, looking shocked.

"Yeah, I went out."

"I didn't think you would!"

"Maybe I could talk to Henry alone," Dr. Denzel suggested.

Sandy bit her lip, then nodded and headed out. "I'll pick up a few more groceries," she offered, "unless you were planning on going out…?"

Henry didn't dignify it with a reply. Sandy left so Henry could talk to the doctor in private. There was a period of silence. Henry waited for the doctor to say something.

"How are you doing, Henry?" Dr. Denzel asked eventually.

"Okay," Henry said quickly, his tone coming out a little belligerent.

"Are you having problems going out?"

Henry shrugged.

"Anxiety attacks, or what? How do you feel when you try to go out?"

"Nervous."

"Yeah? How bad?" he prompted.

"Bad enough I don't go out," Henry said flatly.

"Would you like me to give you something for that?"

"Maybe," he hedged.

"Maybe?" Denzel repeated with a note of surprise.

"What if it affects me other ways—like that other time?"

Dr. Denzel looked puzzled momentarily. Then he remembered what Henry was talking about. "Oh, of course. Well, we will monitor you to make sure it doesn't."

"I don't want it to make me crazy."

"No, of course not. We'll find something that works for you. So you can feel good again."

46

───────

Henry walked along holding Cherise's hand. It had taken them some time to get him back on his feet again. But he was out of his apartment. Trying to reintegrate back into his old life. He looked back over his shoulder again.

"What's wrong?" Cherise asked.

"Nothing," Henry snapped.

"You see someone? What's going on?"

"Nothing. I just—I'm just nervous."

"About what? What's going on?"

"I'm jumpy. That's all. It's nothing."

He looked back over his shoulder again.

"You're making *me* jumpy," Cherise complained.

"Sorry."

She gave him a squeeze with the arm around his waist. "Just relax. You want to go to my place or something?"

"Yeah, let's do that."

They headed back toward Cherise's house. Henry double-checked over his shoulder one more time.

───────

Henry awoke slowly. He was tired and anxious at the same time, disoriented. He went to the bathroom and washed his hands, studying them closely before drying them back off. He put on the coffee machine and pressed Sandy's speed-dial number again. It rang a few times before going to voice mail.

"Where are you?" Henry muttered crossly. He pushed the hang-up button to break the connection. He paced anxiously and decided to go for a walk.

When he got back an hour later, Sandy was in the hall outside his apartment. "I was just looking for you," she offered.

"Where were you?" he growled.

"Working. What's wrong?"

"I don't know. I have the jitters. I have to have something…"

"Drugs?"

"Yeah. Do I ever."

She nodded to the door.

"Let's go in."

Henry nodded and unlocked the door. Sandy took a brief look around, her eyes sharp. She put on fresh coffee and walked around the apartment. Henry put down his newspaper, unable to concentrate on it. Sandy picked it up and flipped through it.

"Look at that," she said, disgusted. Henry looked at her. "Another girl killed. We went through a dry spell there and I thought things were getting better." She concentrated on the text for a minute. "Doesn't say she was a working girl. Found by her parents, it says, so you wouldn't think so. Strangled."

Henry stared at her. "What are you talking about?"

"A girl. Teenager. Strangled. Get with it, Thomas. Man, I thought whoever was doing this had taken off."

"There were others?"

"No one has had the guts to say serial murder yet, but the papers are starting to count up the similar cases. Police won't say anything. Most of the girls are hookers, but they don't say so for this one. I don't recognize the name."

"Oh… I didn't realize."

"It's still third-page news. But *we* pay attention when sickos start killing hookers, even if the cops don't care."

"Were the others strangled?" Henry asked, watching her face.

"A couple. With a rope." Sandy continued to look down at the article, shaking her head. "This one doesn't say how. Maybe they'll publish more details tomorrow."

"Yeah."

They had their coffee in silence while Sandy studied the article and Henry watched her.

Henry looked at the paper after Sandy was gone. The article included the girl's name, but no picture. What they needed was a nice picture of her. Black and white. Soft edges, relaxed, angelic. That's what they needed to really sell the story and make people care. He made a note of the reporter's name.

Maybe he would send her a picture.

47

There was a knock at the door. Henry went to see who it was. He looked through the peephole. Cops. He wet his lips nervously and opened the door.

"Can I help you?" he asked politely.

"Are you Henry Thomson?"

They didn't have anything on him as Henry Thomson. Thomson had no past.

"Yeah."

"We'd like to ask you a few questions."

Henry stepped back to allow them in. "What about?"

They came in and looked around. Henry spotted the open newspaper at the same time as they did.

"You saw the article about Miss Terrence?" His name tag said Aberdene. The other was Bentley.

Henry nodded. "Yeah. I was thinking of going over there… but I've never met her parents. It might be sort of awkward, explaining who I am."

"What would you say?"

"Well, we were friends at school… sort of boyfriend-girlfriend."

"Sort of?" he prompted.

Henry rubbed the back of his neck and shrugged. "Well, how do you tell her folks that we were… you know? Together."

"That you were sleeping with her, you mean?" Aberdene suggested.

Henry nodded.

"She's underage," the cop said, cocking one eyebrow.

"I'm only fifteen," Henry pointed out.

They considered this. "You're fifteen, and you've got your own place?" Aberdene questioned.

"It's a long story."

"You have a baby, like she does."

Henry was surprised. They'd done some homework. He nodded.

"So where is the baby, Henry?"

"I've been sick. Someone else is taking care of him."

"Who?"

Henry gave them the name and phone number.

"And do you have some ID?"

Henry dug out his wallet and showed them his learner's. Bentley dutifully recorded the license number.

"When is the last time you saw Miss Terrence?"

Henry hesitated. Something in their manner suggested they already knew the answer. "A couple of days ago. Before…" he motioned to the paper.

"You saw her the day she was murdered?"

Henry nodded. They just stood there looking at him, waiting.

"I didn't kill her," he said. "We just went to her house. I was nervous… I thought someone was following me."

"Following you?" Aberdene repeated. "What made you think that?"

"I kept seeing this car. A blue wagon with a dented fender."

"Did you see the driver?"

"No."

"Not at all?"

"I thought it was a man."

"White? Black?"

"White."

"How old?"

"I don't know," Henry shrugged widely. "I didn't get a good look."

"A white man in a dented blue wagon. That's all you can tell us?"

"Yeah." He sighed.

"You didn't really see anything, did you? You're just trying to snow us."

"No, I saw it," Henry insisted. He noticed things like that. He didn't used to.

"You and Terrence slept together that day?" Aberdene suggested.

"Yeah."

"You want to provide us with a DNA sample?"

"No."

"A cheek swab is all we need."

"No."

"Why not?"

Henry shrugged and didn't try putting his objection into words. He knew he couldn't give them his DNA.

"You've already admitted you slept with her," Aberdene pointed out.

"Do I need a lawyer?"

Aberdene was silent for a moment. "It might be a good idea."

Henry's stomach flipped. His heart sped up. "Are you arresting me?"

"I think we'd better take you in for questioning."

Henry swallowed, feeling nauseous. Trying to keep himself calm. "No."

"You're refusing to come in?"

Henry didn't know what to do. "I didn't kill her."

"Just come in and talk to us."

"I can't."

"Then call your lawyer. Now."

"I don't have one."

Aberdene reached into his pocket and handed Henry a card. Legal aid numbers. "Can I… have a few minutes?"

"We'll be in the hall."

48

<hr>

At the police station, Henry put his face into his folded arms on the table, burrowing down like he could hibernate and it would all go away. His new lawyer, Mr. Brampton, and the cops had stepped out into the hallway to talk, but they hadn't shut the door all the way. Maybe they meant for him to hear.

"He's already admitted to sleeping with her. Why not give a DNA sample?" Aberdene asked impatiently.

"If he's admitted to it, why do you need one?" Brampton asked, his tone reasonable.

"Simply to corroborate his story."

"You're not looking to corroborate his story. You're looking to hang him."

"This kid is up to his eyeballs in trouble. You don't think we believe the line that they were being followed that day?"

"Have you checked into it?" Brampton countered.

"We will, but you know it's a red herring.

"You've got no evidence that my client has done anything."

"The girl was murdered in her own bed. She let the murderer in."

240

"Or a door was left unlocked. Or the murderer jimmied it. Or someone else with a key let him in."

"I want to know if your client used protection."

There was silence for a moment from Brampton. Henry's heart pounded in his ears, filling the silence. "Why?"

"We want to know if he was the last one with her. What if the DNA is someone else's? It could clear him if she was with someone else after him."

"I need time to talk to my client in private."

"Go ahead. We've got some calls to make."

The door swung open the rest of the way and Brampton came in. "Henry." He shook Henry's shoulder hard. "Come on, Henry. We have to talk."

Henry roused himself and rubbed his eyes.

"We need a strategy, here, buddy. You need to fill me in on a few things."

"What?" Henry questioned groggily, rubbing his eyes and yawning.

"You and the victim were intimate before she was murdered."

"Yeah, I told them that. She was my girlfriend."

"This is very important. Did you use a condom?"

"No."

"So, it's your DNA they're going to find."

"Yeah."

"Then you may as well submit to a DNA test. It doesn't really harm our case. They know it was you. We know it was you. That doesn't mean it was murder. I mean, it wasn't rape, right? You weren't rough."

Henry shook his head. "No, I'd never do that."

"There was no violence. They can't positively link the murder to you."

Henry shook his head. "I can't give them a sample," he insisted.

"It's just a cheek swab. Nothing embarrassing."

"I can't. Trust me."

Brampton studied Henry. Henry dropped his eyes down to the top of the table.

"Even if you committed the murder—and you don't have to tell me if you did—I still don't see a problem with them doing the DNA test," Brampton said.

"What if they use it for something else?" Henry said nervously.

Brampton frowned. "For something else..." he frowned, shaking his head. "Well, what are the odds that they would run it against anything else?"

Henry was silent. Brampton stared at him for a few minutes, then finally nodded. "If it's too much of a risk. We'll fight it the best we can. But they may force the issue in court. There's not much we can do if the court orders you to provide a sample."

Henry nodded.

He held onto the fact that they didn't have anything on him. They only had suspicions.

Henry was waiting for Brampton to come back and tell him he was free to go back to his apartment. Aberdene walked in instead. He looked around, frowning.

"Where's your lawyer?"

"He went to find you," Henry told him.

"Well, I just got back from searching your apartment."

Henry thought he would faint. He had the sensation of free fall. Like he'd been dropped down into a bottomless pit. How had they gotten a warrant to search his apartment? His stomach dropped. The rushing wind filled his ears. His heart expanded to fill his chest until he thought it would burst with fear. He couldn't swallow, couldn't speak. Could hardly breathe. He had to go to the bathroom.

Brampton walked back in.

"I've been looking for you," Aberdene said impatiently.

Brampton took in Henry's frozen, panicked expression. "What's going on?"

"Your client is under arrest. Explain his rights to him."

"You don't have enough for an arrest," Brampton countered.

"We didn't, but we had enough for a search warrant for his apartment. Maybe your client would like to tell you what we found there."

Everyone looked at Henry, who just sat there wide-eyed and white-faced. Aberdene started pulling out photos and dropping them on the table. Brampton waited for someone to explain further.

"Photos from his apartment. All of these lovely girls," Aberdene said, "have been murdered in the last year."

Brampton swore. "Don't say anything," he told Henry.

Henry sat there frozen, unable to speak or even move.

"A bunch of kiddie porn in the darkroom," Aberdeen went on, laying them out.

Henry averted his eyes. He had to do something to make a living. At least it was photography.

Aberdene put some syringes on the table. "A heroin addiction," he commented.

Henry didn't even know there were still needles at the apartment, let alone any heroin. Sandy had gone through it before he got back from rehab to make sure he couldn't shoot up as soon as he got home. How had she missed it?

Aberdene put some orange plastic prescription bottles on the table. "I'm told these are powerful antipsychotics."

Everybody just stood there, stunned, staring at Henry.

"How about a confession, Henry?" Aberdene prompted. "You know you're caught."

"Don't say anything," Brampton said automatically.

Henry looked at the pictures. Adrienne, Cherise, and all the others. So pretty. His girls.

There had been two Henrys for too long. The thrill-seeker and the cover.

He used to be the cover. A good kid. Responsible. Naive. Victimized.

But that Henry had slowly been consumed by the other. The predator that lurked beneath, getting off on risk-taking and breaking the rules.

The Henry that had once been buried deep had surfaced day by day until the other Henry was barely a paper mask he kept between the predator and the world.

He had tried to hide the evil, bury it, forget the things it did. But it had been stronger. Where did it come from?

Frank had tried to tell him about it, to explain it. They were both victims of an awful monster that lurked inside.

But no. Henry rejected this.

He was a survivor. The Henry who lived and grew stronger wasn't a victim.

The Henry who was a victim was gone, overcome by the stronger one.

Henry reached tentatively for the pictures. No-one stopped him. He gathered them into a pile and pulled them to him. He fingered them tenderly, stroking the lovely faces.

"They're so beautiful," he murmured.

"Then why kill them?" Aberdene questioned.

This time Brampton didn't jump in and tell him to be quiet. Even he wanted to know.

"I loved to follow them. Take candids. Watch them at work or at home. But you can't do that forever. People notice you and get suspicious."

"And if you can't have them, no one can?" Aberdene suggested.

"Yes, there's that," Henry admitted. "But also… the high…" he hesitated, "the rush…?"

Aberdene nodded understandingly, sympathetically.

He understood. Someone understood.

Henry sighed, the tension draining away.

There was no more need to hide who he really was. No more mask.

Henry was what he was.

EPILOGUE

Sandy was sitting on a park bench, pouring over the newspaper.

"Like seeing your boyfriend in the paper?" a voice said over her shoulder. Sandy startled and turned to look at Marty.

"He's not my boyfriend," Sandy said firmly. She stared at the article. "I can't believe he killed those girls," she mused. "Do you think he really did it, John?"

Marty chuckled. "Sure, why not?"

"He's just not the type. He's a nerdy, shy kid. I was surprised he was even going out with anyone."

"He's a lot of things besides being shy and nerdy. He was in juvie for murder, you know."

"Yeah, well, someone else confessed to that one."

"Doesn't mean Specs didn't do it."

"He's had trouble, but I thought he was basically a straight arrow."

"A straight arrow who was hooked on heroin."

"Not really his fault. It started as morphine after your boys beat him up."

"Because he killed my lieutenant."

Sandy was shocked. She looked at him. "What?"

"He killed Richie. Why, I don't know. He didn't like having the pinch put on him, I guess. He was also making porn and using a false ID."

"And he shoplifted for thrills," Sandy admitted. "But—what makes you think Thomas killed Richards?"

"Well, it wasn't Katya, was it? They had a lover's quarrel and she stabbed him in the gut and then lugged him to the basement? I don't think so. And it wasn't Hans; he doesn't have the guts. That just leaves Specs."

"And you think he could do that? Stab Richards to death? Be calm and cool enough to clean up any evidence and dispose of the body?"

"I saw him drill a guard in juvie and not even turn a hair."

Sandy pushed her red hair back from her face, tucking it over one ear. "You're putting me on."

"No. He's been doing it all along, Sandy. But no one will believe it when they look into his shy-owl face."

"How many people has he killed?" Sandy breathed.

"I bet if you take the number in the paper and double it, you're probably in the ballpark."

"That's—unbelievable."

Marty nodded. "He's got a good cover. You want to know why serial killers go so long without getting caught, it's 'cause they look like him."

Sandy shook her head, looking at the paper without really seeing it. She closed her eyes and rubbed them with her palms, trying to massage away her headache. "The cops called me about him."

Marty sat down on the bench. "Why?"

"Well… they called his doctor, the one who prescribed all of his meds. He couldn't say much to them, but he knew me because I brought him to Thomas's apartment once when he was all screwed up and couldn't leave his apartment. Sure wish I hadn't done that; I might have saved that girl's life. Anyway, the doctor had my number down as an emergency contact."

"What did the cops want to know?"

Sandy looked at Marty, biting her lip. "When they saw me… they recognized me."

He was unsurprised. "From where, vice?"

"Thomas had taken pictures of me. Pictures like he had of all those other girls."

"He was stalking you?"

"They said I might have been next on his list. He was following me around. Taking pictures of me working, tele-photos through windows while I was changing, all kinds of stalker stuff."

Marty shook his head. "Whack-job. What is it they say? Still waters?"

"Yeah."

Sandy slowly closed the paper, shaking her head.

———

Sandy's story continues in *Sandy, Breaking the Pattern*

Did you enjoy this book? Reviews and recommendations are vital to making a book successful.

Please leave a review at your favorite book store or review site and share it with your friends.

Don't miss the following bonus material:
Sign up for mailing list to get a free ebook
Read a sneak preview chapter
Other books by P.D. Workman
Learn more about the author

Sign up for my mailing list at pdworkman.com and get Gluten-Free Murder for free!

PREVIEW OF SANDY

BREAKING THE PATTERN #2

CHAPTER 1

Sun streamed through the dingy windows of the hospital onto the white sheets of the bed and curtains. Mol held the squalling pink bundle out to Rene. Rene took the baby and jiggled her, gazing down at her. She had a fuzz of rusty orange hair covering her head. Her eyes, though blue, were dark, shifting a little under the light, making him think that they would turn out to be green or brown.

"She has a healthy cry," he observed, "no?"

"Very," Mol agreed, wincing. "Now, you tell me now if you're going to look after her, because I'll just give her up if not."

He shook his head. "No, I will look after her."

"How can you look after her? What do you know about babies?" Molly demanded.

The baby's sobs were gradually slowing as he jiggled her.

"I know all about feeding and changing. What else is there?" Rene said flippantly.

"Plenty. And don't you be calling me every time you have a problem. One kid is more than enough for me. I'm not going back to diapers."

"I won't call you," he promised.

"Good."

Rene looked down at the baby girl. She had stopped crying and her stormy eyes stared at him with a focus and intensity far too old and wise for a newborn. Rene gave her a satisfied smile.

"I have big plans for you, little girl," he promised. "Big plans."

———

A couple of years later, Mol saw Rene at the grocery store. Usually, they just ignored each other, but this time he approached her.

"Good morning, Molly," he greeted politely.

"Rene."

"That's her," Rene said to the solemn little redheaded toddler sitting in his shopping cart. "That's your mom."

"Oh."

Mol looked at Rene with a frown.

"What's all this about, then?" she questioned.

"She's been asking who her mom is."

Mol looked at Sandy for a moment and shrugged.

"Whatever."

Years would pass before Molly would voice to Sandy her regret that she had ever put Sandy into Rene's custody.

CHAPTER 2

S andy watched herself in the mirror as she brushed her long red hair. She assessed herself critically, studying her hair, makeup, and outfit. Examining her legs and stomach for any extra weight, carefully evaluating everything. Her pager went off, and she silenced it without looking and finished brushing her hair. Sandy put down the brush and looked at the number on her pager. She didn't recognize it.

She really should be hitting the street, but she shrugged off the momentary guilt at delaying, and made the call.

"Sandy?" an unfamiliar male voice queried.

"Who's this?" she questioned.

"It's Dr. Denzel."

Sandy swallowed. Henry had given her name to Denzel as his emergency contact.

"Is Henry okay?" she questioned.

"He's well... but he's in some trouble." Denzel sounded grave.

"What for? Drugs?"

"No... it's worse than that."

"What?"

"There are some officers who would like to talk to you. They want to talk to people who know Henry. You're the only one I know about."

"Okay. It's pretty bad, huh?" Sandy questioned, her voice catching.

"Yes. Do you want an officer to pick you up, or—"

"I'll get there on my own. What precinct? Downtown?"

"Yes. Ask for Aberdene."

"Okay. I'll be there."

Sandy ended the call and stood there wondering what Henry had managed to get himself into. She assessed her outfit and decided she'd better tone it down. After slipping out of the mini skirt into a pair of blue jeans and pulling a crocheted sweater over the midi, she picked up the phone again and called Marcia.

"Hey, Sandy," Marcia greeted.

"Hi, Marcia. Listen, I'm not gonna be out today."

"You sick or slacking off?" Marcia challenged.

"Got a last-minute call."

"Okay, girl. Thanks for letting me know."

"Yeah. See you tomorrow."

———

Sandy stood around waiting for Aberdene. He eventually showed up, looking around and picking her out.

"Sandy?"

"Yeah." She looked at his name tag, which designated him a detective.

"So, what's Thomas got himself into?" she questioned.

"You know him by his real name," he observed.

Sandy shrugged. Thomson. He was Henry Thomson now. He was always reminding her.

"Come sit down with me, we'll talk," Aberdene invited.

Sandy went along with him. She caught him looking at her sidelong a couple of times. She looked to see whether all of her buttons were done up, and then ignored his looks. He took her to a conference room and sat her down. They were joined by another detective named Bentley. Sandy saw startled recognition in his eyes. She didn't recognize him; but she met many men and only really remembered the regulars.

"So, what's this about?" she questioned again.

"Your friend Henry is under arrest for murder," Aberdeen said.

It was so completely unexpected, Sandy wasn't able to suppress a gasp at the information.

"Murder?" she repeated in disbelief. "You've got the wrong guy!"

"What makes you think that?"

"He's a nerd. He's not the kind to kill someone!"

"He's confessed."

"Henry? Who would he kill?"

Bentley slid a photo across the table toward her. Sandy looked at the picture of the blond. A candid shot, soft edges, glamorous.

"Is that one of Henry's photos?"

Bentley nodded. Sandy studied her face. "I've never met her. Was she… his girlfriend? Or a stranger?"

"Girlfriend."

"The one from school?"

They both nodded.

"Why? Why would he kill her?" Sandy still couldn't believe it. Not Henry. She knew a lot of guys who were violent, who she wouldn't doubt for a minute could kill. But Henry? That baby face?

"This one… we're not quite sure why," Aberdene said. "The others… it appears that people started to get suspicious, noticed him hanging around where he shouldn't be."

"The others?" Sandy repeated.

Bentley shifted his seat forward.

"There were others," he confirmed.

Sandy swallowed. She looked from one cop to the other.

"He's not a killer," she affirmed. "He hasn't been killing girls." Then suddenly, everything connected and Sandy felt nauseated. "Oh, no…!"

They waited for her to go on. Sandy cleared her throat, trying to keep her voice steady.

"Don't tell me he's the one… who's been strangling working girls…"

"What makes you suggest that?" Bentley questioned sharply.

"There hasn't been any other series of unsolved murders, has there?"

"Even those girls haven't been identified as a series," Aberdene pointed out. "How do you know about that?"

"Because I'm in the business," Sandy said in exasperation, "and we notice when other girls are being killed, even if no one else does. So, is he the one? Is he the one killing them?"

Aberdene nodded, looking grim. "Yes, he's the one."

Bentley laid down a series of other photos on the table. Sandy touched a couple of them.

"Katelyn… Josie… are you sure Henry did this?"

"He has their pictures. They're dead. He admits it."

Sandy swore; she couldn't believe it. How could it be him?

"Henry has had two other prior murder charges, you know," Aberdene pointed out.

"Two? I only knew about one. He was in juvie with my brother—but someone else confessed to it."

They shrugged.

"He got lucky," Bentley said. "Twice. But this time…"

Sandy shook her head. "I just… can't believe it."

"We'd like to ask you some background questions about Henry, okay?" Aberdene said.

Bentley held up his hand. "Hang on one sec," he told Aberdene, and delved into his portfolio, looking for another series of pictures. He shuffled through them, and pulled a few out, handing them to Sandy.

Sandy looked down at pictures of herself. Her stomach lurched. They were pictures she never knew Henry had taken. Head shots, full length, pictures through her window, down the street, laughing with a friend, meeting a client, even one of her shooting up, totally unaware she was being observed. He must have used a telephoto lens.

"You could have been next," Bentley said.

"I never knew he was taking those," Sandy said. Her stomach lurched, and she put her hand over it. "Oh man… I'm gonna be sick…"

Aberdene stood up. "Let's take a break. I'll show you to the restroom."

"Yeah. Thanks."

———

Sandy splashed water on her face and took a few deep breaths, trying to settle her nerves and clear her mind. So what if Henry Thomas was a serial killer?

It wasn't as if they were that close to each other. He'd never been her type. He was a loser. Sure, she'd taken him under her wing when he was hurt and sick, she felt sorry for him and his baby brother. He didn't have anyone else.

That was all over. He was going away for a long time now.

Sandy stepped out of the room and looked around. Aberdene was talking to another cop and made a sign indicating that he'd be with her in a couple of minutes. Dr. Denzel was sitting in a lobby at the end of the hall and Sandy walked down to talk to him. He looked as sick and gray as Sandy felt. He saw her and stood up to shake her hand.

"Sandy—how are you?"

"Well—in shock, I guess. I just… I had no idea."

Denzel nodded. They sat down.

"Henry told me," Denzel said, pain in his eyes.

"He did? Today?"

"No… when he was at the clinic."

Sandy stared at him in shock. Denzel knew back then, months ago?

"He was on a new medication when he told me," Denzel explained further. "He was uninhibited, his associations were very loose. I thought it was a psychotic break."

Sandy shook her head wordlessly.

"I didn't believe him," Denzel said. "I thought it was his imagination. A hallucination."

"You couldn't have known."

"I should have known. I should have paid closer attention. Seen the warning signs."

"How could anyone have known?" Sandy protested. "I even talked to him about them! About the girls getting killed. He never acted suspiciously."

"I knew more about him than anyone. I knew his family history… his mom's mental illness and her tendency to pick abusive partners… I knew all her worries about him, but he always seemed like such a responsible, mature kid… I never took her concerns seriously…"

He put his face in his hands, shaking his head and breathing raggedly.

Sandy sat there wondering what she could say or do to comfort him. She understood the guilt. She felt it too. They sat in silence, both at a loss, in shock over the development.

Sandy, Breaking the Pattern, Book #2 of the *Breaking the Pattern* series by P.D. Workman can be purchased at pdwork-man.com

ABOUT THE AUTHOR

Award-winning and USA Today bestselling author P.D. (Pamela) Workman writes riveting mystery/suspense and young adult books dealing with mental illness, addiction, abuse, and other real-life issues. For as long as she can remember, the blank page has held an incredible allure and from a very young age she was trying to write her own books.

Workman wrote her first complete novel at the age of twelve and continued to write as a hobby for many years. She started publishing in 2013. She has won several literary awards from Library Services for Youth in Custody for her young adult fiction. She currently has over 70 published titles and can be found at pdworkman.com.

Born and raised in Alberta, Workman has been married for over 25 years and has one son.

———

Please visit P.D. Workman at pdworkman.com to see what else she is working on, to join her mailing list, and to link to her social networks.

———

If you enjoyed this book, please take the time to recommend it to other purchasers with a review or star rating and share it with your friends!

facebook.com/pdworkmanauthor

twitter.com/pdworkmanauthor

instagram.com/pdworkmanauthor

amazon.com/author/pdworkman

bookbub.com/authors/p-d-workman

goodreads.com/pdworkman

linkedin.com/in/pdworkman

pinterest.com/pdworkmanauthor

youtube.com/pdworkman

9 781774 682012